FLIRTING IN GOOD FAITH

by
Gaurav Narang

An Imprint of
B. Jain Publishers (P) Ltd.
An ISO 9001 : 2000 Certified Company
USA – EUROPE – INDIA

FLIRTING IN GOOD FAITH

First Edition: 2009

All rights reserved. No part of this book may be reproduced, stored in a retrieval system or transmitted, in any form or by any means, mechanical, photocopying, recording or otherwise, without any prior written permission of the publisher.

© with the author

Published by Kuldeep Jain for

Pegasus
An imprint of
B. JAIN PUBLISHERS (P) LTD.
An ISO 9001 : 2000 Certified Company
1921/10, Chuna Mandi, Paharganj, New Delhi 110 055 (INDIA)
Tel.: 91-11-2358 0800, 2358 1100, 2358 1300, 2358 3100
Fax: 91-11-2358 0471 • *Email:* info@bjain.com
Website: **www.bjainbooks.com**

Printed in India by
J.J. Offset Printers

ISBN: 978-81-319-0661-3

Publisher's Note

We continue our venture into high-quality fiction with "*Flirting in Good Faith*" by Gaurav Narang being about young adults of the urban upper middle class, their dreams and aspirations and their emotional entanglements as seen through the eyes of a small town dweller who migrates to the Big City to improve his life chances. As the narrative unfolds, the reader is given a refreshing insight into the carefree lives and concerns of a small group of students which nevertheless has its anxieties and insecurities as well. The novel's main characters give us a glimpse of IIM life, the occasional discotheque dancing, affairs of the heart and above all a saga of unrequited love and academic failure of the narrator and prime protagonist.

The novel comes at a time when GenX is attracting nationwide star billing in the print media, and the hopes and expectations from the idealism and energy of the young generation – now a majority – that a people have for changing the face of Indo-Anglian literature, popular music, the sporting arena and above all, of leadership.

The growing expectations reflect the ever-spreading disillusionment with the older generation and its universally resented propensity to stick to conservatism and convention and its proven poor track record. *"Flirting in Good Faith"* mirrors an era of a people's desperate search for youngsters who, in Ratan Tata's memorable words, *"rock the boat"*. We need unconventional young adults who have moral courage, vision, perseverance, virtue and who are not bound by traditional ways and who are highly motivated to do their best.

Kuldeep Jain
C.E.O., B. Jain Publishers (P) Ltd.

Preface

When my publishers suggested me to write a preface for this book, the first thing I did was to google out what a preface should contain. It should tell why the book was written? I did give it a thought for a week or so and finally I am convinced that I have not written this story for any specific reason. I have written it just because I enjoy the process of writing.

This is not the story of a hero; there are no guns and explosions, no magic, no deities, no mysteries even. It is simply a story of a normal human being; much like you and me. He does not always know what he wants yet he always enjoy every moment of his life. He does not live for any specific purpose yet he always makes each small aspiration a purpose in itself. He often contradicts himself and he is not afraid to do that.

As you read this story, don't expect anything supernatural. Just read it lightly and somewhere you will find the connection, somewhere you might realize that this is your own story.

Gaurav Narang

Acknowledgements

It is always a difficult task to write acknowledgements for you never know whom you might upset. However my first regards should definitely go to the person who encouraged me to write this book, who told me that people will read this book and any publisher would be willing to accept it. Had he not forced me to approach a publishing house this book would not be in your hands. He is my best critic and friend Vishal Haria.

Apart from Vishal, I would like to express my gratitude towards my family members who always had faith in me and always encouraged me to try different things including writing this book. I would like to thank all my friends who have always been there for me.

Last and the most important, I would express my regards to my publishers Pegasus* who accepted my manuscript and assisted me throughout the process of completing this story.

After mailing them an incomplete sample I had forgotten about the book altogether. If it was not for their acceptance I might not have thought of completing the book itself.

Gaurav Narang

ent
FRIENDS FOREVER

I

"You are my first and last love; I will never be able to love anyone ever again in my life." She was the fourth girl to whom I had told that, but somehow this time I felt different, this time I was confident, this time I could feel the sincerity in my words, this time I knew I was talking to the girl who was going to be my wife and this time I was much more sure than I was ever before on the earlier occasions.

The first thing I had noticed about Anisha was her irritating voice. It was around three years ago, my first day in college when I noticed this girl with shrill voice and it took only five seconds for me to develop an instinctive dislike for her which was reciprocated with equal intensity by Anisha over an extended period of time. Wearing a blue kameez and white salwar she looked as if she had walked straight out of a village school. There were ten characters of female species in the class of fifty engineering students and then there was Anisha. Though no one ever claimed that she belonged to the female species but no one ever counter claimed either. As for Anisha it did not matter because she belongs to a very rare species known in intellectual parlance as 'aloof' species. Irrespective of everything it was imperative for me to approach her and introduce myself; a ritual I never failed to perform. "Hi, I am Satyam" I started the talk. "Your zip is open," she replied humbly. What made me hate her was not the fact which she had stated so sweetly but the realization that she had stated that fact in presence of ten other females making sure that my celibacy lasts a little longer than I had initially planned. I did the best thing that anyone could do in such a situation, I zipped up and then I did the worst thing that anyone could do in such a situation, I completed the ritual by offering her a handshake. "Hi, I am Satyam again." She looked at me in such disgust as if it was her and not me who had zipped my jeans. It was just then that the faculty entered the classroom and with everyone occupying whatever seats they could, I sat next to Anisha.

The first lecture was of Engineering Mathematics. Professor Romesh Ganguly was a Bengali. He had a petite frame and receding hairline, must be in his mid sixties. Given by the structure of his body it seemed like either he suffered from acute diarrhoea or he had learnt his lessons from the Bengal Famine and had been preparing himself for the next one all these years. He was wearing a light blue half sleeve shirt and neatly pressed khaki trousers with matching sandals.

This was the moment I had been waiting for, first class of graduation. How different it would be from school.... how much independence...... how much fun..... Different, indeed it was. Adjusting his glasses the professor said, "My name is Romesh Ganguly, you can call me RG. I am not interested in knowing your names, primarily because I would not remember them and secondly because with so much to cover I will never have time to interact with any of you." He paused, "How many of you are not carrying your textbooks?" No hand rose. "How many of you are carrying your textbook?" he changed the question. A few hands rose this time. "From tomorrow onwards no one will be allowed in my class without the textbook. We will end today's class here. Everyone should solve practice exercise of Chapter one and get it signed by me tomorrow" with these words he left the class. There was a pin drop silence which lasted for about two minutes until some of the guys realized their priorities. Coming back to reality they started chatting with girls again.

"Hi, I am Satyam again," I said. "Anisha," she replied. It seemed like she didn't want to talk but determined to continue the conversation I asked "Are you virgin?" To this date I don't know why I said that or what I was thinking when I said that but the damage was already done. "What sort of question is that?" she yelled. Her yelling lead to something which I had often dreamt of and which would have taken many accomplishments to achieve. With all eyes fixated on us, suddenly I was the center of attraction. Not experienced in handling such kind of lime light before I said meekly, "All I meant to ask was if you have a boyfriend." "And why do you bother about that?" she continued yelling. By now I had realized that no one knew why she had started shouting on me and so there was no need for me to be soft and anyway there were other girls who were now intently watching me and who needed to be impressed. Raising my voice I replied, "This was out of concern, just wanted to tell you that if you will always be this rude you will never get a boy friend." Having delivered the blow I turned my back towards Anisha and started walking back when someone lightly tapped my shoulder. I turned back to find it was Anisha, she yelled again her voice louder than before, "thanks for your concern but leave me alone." "Isn't that what I was exactly doing when I had started to move? And you also stay away from me," I added as I left the classroom and this set the tone of our relationship.

We did not talk to each other for almost a year until one day Avash told me that he loved Anisha. Though Avash had always been a strange character with weird interests but his interest in Anisha was beyond my wildest expectations. It came more as a shock than a surprise. At 6 feet 2 inches Avash was taller than anyone else in the batch, he had got looks of a model and at times it felt like he had hired his brain from Einstein. God has his own way of maintaining balance, where he gave Avash everything a girl would desire he purposely rewarded Avash with a lot of gentleness, loads of honesty and very little amount of confidence making sure he never gets a girl friend. It was hard to believe that a guy like Avash will stoop so low to get interested in Anisha, on the contrary it seemed as if he was interested in Anisha because she appeared to be the easiest catch among all the females of our batch.

This was the time for me to show the right path to Avash and I tried my best to bring him to his senses but to no avail. I tried to influence him to consider other girls in the class but most of them were already booked and even to me Anisha did seem like the easiest catch. Avash stuck to the point that he loved Anisha not because she was the easiest catch but because of some metaphysical reasons which I would not understand. For the next two years I felt that Avash was lying to me since no one could ever love Anisha but finally I realized he was telling the truth all this time. This realization came after I found out that I myself was in love with Anisha and that changed the course of my life. That day, I gave up my long cherished aim of becoming the Prime Minister of this country and the world lost a great leader.

2

"I Love you." I told her again in a plain voice bereft of any emotions. Emotions dilute facts. When stating a fact one need not be emotional. I loved her and that was a fact which I repeated in a calm voice. Long silence ensued which was broken by a loud thud; the voice of someone's hand against someone's cheek, Anisha's hand and my cheek. She slapped me and then she hugged me and started crying. This was the first time she had slapped me and this was the first time she had hugged me. Numerous emotions ran through my mind, many questions unanswered. What did that mean? Did she love me? Why did she slap me? Why is she now hugging me? Why is she crying? Is this the end of our friendship? Will I be able to live without her? Is it because she loves Avash? Does she actually love Avash?

When Avash had first told me about his feelings for Anisha there was nothing between them. They were not even good friends. Thanks to his shy nature Avash could never gather enough courage to talk to her for a while. "You have got to help me out, I love her," Avash had told me. I however was not interested in building any sort of communication with Anisha. "You are my best friend. You are the only one I can trust. I know you don't like her but I can not do it without you. You know I will never have the guts to approach her myself. You have got to help me out. You have to do this for our friendship. You have got to help me out, I love her" Avash repeated. I relented; after all that happened in the first year, even I had to settle my score with her. That night Avash stayed back at my hostel. We went to 'Cumsum plaza'. Whole night he kept talking about her and I kept on thinking about a plan to take my revenge with her. By morning, I had the rough idea of what seemed like a sound plan.

It was Friday, the last working day of college before our end semester exams which were scheduled from Monday. The first paper was engineering mathematics, the subject which had always troubled mere mortals like Anisha and me. Avash was exceptionally good at quantitative stuff and this was the central point of my plan. During lunch break when the class was empty I went to Anisha's seat and took out her math book. Next lecture was of mathematics and Professor RG did not allow Anisha to attend the class. She felt hurt and I was happy. I had taken my revenge.

After college was over Anisha started walking back to bus stop in a dejected mood. This was the right opportunity for me to implement the next step of my plan. "What has happened to you Anisha? You seem to be a little upset," I asked as I approached her. Avash was standing by my side. She took a few moments to digest who had approached her, looked at me scornfully and replied "None of your business." The look she gave me was not because she suspected me of stealing her book but it was a look born out of deep disregard for each other which we had developed over the year and which both of us had always cherished. "Anisha I know you don't like me. I know what you think of me but still we are classmates. We have at least three more years to spend in the same class. I saw you were very upset and so I approached you thinking I might be of some help but probably I was wrong. I am sorry but I only wanted to help. I am sorry," I said in the most humble voice I could and started walking back slowly. I knew it had to work and it did. "I lost my math book", she told calmly. "You must have forgotten it at your home. Don't worry," I suggested. "No. I remember I brought it, in fact I was reading it on my way to college. I must have lost it somewhere. I don't know" she said. "That's bad. How will you study for exam now?" I asked sounding as genuine as was humanly possible for me. She looked down, waited for a while and said "I don't know." She started walking back again. The time to strike had come. "Anisha if you want you can join us. Avash and I always study together. He is good at math. We will be able to manage with two books and Avash will help us prepare well", I said slowly giving her sufficient time to digest the whole thing. She thought for a while, looked down then looked up and was still thinking when Avash intervened, "It will be fine Anisha, you can study with us. I have already solved most of the problems and it will not take long." "Thanks for your help. I will call you if I need any help", she said and she left. The plan had taken off well.

"Isn't it strange? We approached her at the perfect time. Thank God!" said Avash. He seemed to be unusually happy and why shouldn't he be? After all he was going to sit for hours with his love. "There is no one called God. Nothing happens by chance. It was all planned." I replied as I handed out Anisha's book to Avash. A triumphant smile crossed my lips. "You stole it......" Avash said looking at me in disbelief. "No, I did not steal it. I have taken it for a few days so that you two can come close and I will put it back in her bag after the exams get over. It's as simple as that" I replied. It was Avash's turn to once again start the non ending debate of ethics and virtues, rights and wrongs. "It is not that simple Satyam. I love her. I can not base the foundation of my love on a lie. What if she gets to know about it tomorrow? What will happen then?" Avash asked. "First tell me what your concern is? Is it that what we are doing is not right or is it what if she gets to know about it?" I asked rather bluntly which I always do to cut these discussions short. Avash kept silent for a while and then asked in a very mild tone, "What if she gets to know about it? She will leave me then." "And how my dear friend will she get to know about it? It is only between you and me. No one else knows of it. So don't bother about it" I replied. Avash did not argue further. We left Anisha's book at my hostel and then went to Avash's home which becomes my base during exam times.

Avash had a big flat in a multistorey apartment in Kailash Colony. His parents were settled in States. They made sure that Avash never feels their absence by providing him with all the luxuries money could buy. To add to that there was a hefty check that he received every month towards his monthly expenses. During day time Avash used to stay in my hostel room, going back to his home after dark, only to catch some sleep. However during the exam week we made it a point to stay at his place as there were servants to take care of all our needs and we could apply our full concentration on studies. His flat was on the third floor with the main gate leading to the hall and two rooms each on either side of the hall. The rooms on left were being used by the servants while the rooms on right were Avash's bedroom and study. With five wooden closets lying along the back wall, his study room looked like a mini library. There were two computer tables, one each placed along the left and the right wall. In the centre there was a circular conference table with six reclining chairs made of Italian leather.

We had just taken our seats at the table when Avash's phone rang. It was Anisha. She told Avash that she would be coming in half an hour. Though he had taken a bath just two hours ago Avash again took a quick shower and dressed up in his favourite blue jeans and white T-shirt. The way he was grooming himself it seemed as if he was preparing for his marriage and not for a study session but then, people do go nuts in love and Avash was no exception. As far as I am concerned I was still dressed in my night suit and having taken a bath just one day ago there was no question of wasting any more water. Though Avash did want me to make an exception this time but I explained to him our responsibility towards water conservation and how I would have to sacrifice one more day of bath now in order to compensate on his extravagant second bath of the day. We were still having our discussion on how India's water problem can be solved just by bathing on alternate days when the door bell rang.

Wearing a black skirt and brown top Anisha looked as weird to me as she had looked on the first day of college. Ignoring me completely she said hi to Avash and occupied the chair on his right. I was sitting towards his left. As Avash started explaining the concepts I could observe a grave change in him. His voice had suddenly become sweet, suddenly he was explaining everything twice, suddenly he forgot that even I needed to understand the problems, however I can not blame him for this; didn't I mention that people do go nuts in love. Avash had just explained a problem when I asked him to explain it for a second time and then a third time not because I had not understood it but to make him realize my presence. Though Avash did not suspect anything but Anisha understood and smiled slowly. I smiled back. Slowly all three of us started talking and studying. By end of day we had developed a little comfort level with each other. As we were about to pack up I spoke, "I am sorry for what happened during our first meeting, let us patch up." Anisha did not reply. "It means you have still not forgiven me?" I asked. "No, not that; but before we patch up I would want to ask you something," Anisha said gravely. Already feeling embarrassed I kept quite as she finally asked, "Are you virgin?" I was dumbfounded as both of them started laughing together. When the laughter did not stop, I joined them too.

Finally, the plan had succeeded. The group studying that we had initially planned for mathematics exam only got extended to other exams as well and that was the period when we three started developing a common bond. That was the period when Avash and Anisha started coming close to each other. But did Anisha actually love him?

3

Not knowing what to do, I once again stated the plain fact, "I love you." She was still crying and she was still hugging me. I went on, "I do not know whether I should be saying all this or not. I know Avash loves you. I know even you have a soft corner for him. I know he trusts me blindly but still I have to share my feelings with you. I have to let you know that I am in love with you. That is all I have to say." She stepped back and wiped her tears. "Let us go and have coffee," she said and started walking. I started following her quietly, wondering how I had landed up in that soup.

After our exams were over we started staying together in college and as time progressed we became very good friends. Most of the times the three of us were together and whenever we were not Avash made it a point not to discuss anything about Anisha with me. He told me it was because he was still not convinced if his feelings towards her were of love or just infatuation and he wanted to find it out himself. I have never been able to understand how people can put so much trust on themselves. What they have not been able to discover in one month how can they be sure that they will discover it some day and when will that destined day come, one month or two months or one year or may be never. "It can only be one of the two things, either you know what you are or you don't, either you know you are in love or you know you are not. How can you leave it to the unknown to discover something for you and what that unknown is?" I had argued with Avash. "May be destiny," he replied. "What destiny? Do you think whether the God or the destiny has any time to bother about whether Avash loves Anisha or not? Is there a switch somewhere which the destiny will turn on one day to tell you "hey Avash! See it is green you can now go forward and propose to her?" or are you waiting for an akashwani or something?" I asked. Probably Avash did not like my tone or I guess he felt I was making fun of his feelings. He left without replying and after that we never discussed Anisha however it did not have any effect on our friendship and we three had a great time through out the second year.

Our third year classes had just begun. Early morning 2 AM on Saturday I received a call. It was Anisha, she was crying. "Hey! Why are you crying dear?" I asked. Instead of replying she continued to cry and I was unable to understand what to say or do as I had no clue of why she was crying; also, I wanted to sleep. She kept weeping for some time after which she finally spoke, "Avash proposed to me" and she started crying again. It came more as a shock than a surprise, not because Avash did not inform me earlier but because I had never expected Avash to have the guts to propose to someone. "Hey! That's great news, Congratulations!" I said. I was feeling very happy for both of them. "Stop this drama now *yaar*, just let me know when you people are treating me and remember both of you will have to treat me separately," I said. However Anisha was still crying as she finally spoke, "Satyam, I have lost my best friend today." "Yes you have, but this is because he is your buddy now, right?" I asked. "Wrong" she added, "Avash has cheated me," and she started crying again. I was not able to understand what she meant? How can Avash ever cheat her or for that matter anyone, he was most unsophisticated and honest person I had ever met. Unable to understand anything I said, "Anisha please don't cry, go have a glass of water and then tell me in detail what has happened otherwise I would not be able to understand anything that you say." She composed herself and then asked, "Do you remember how we people had started studying together?" "Yes," I replied. "It was Avash who had stolen my book," she said, and then she kept quite. She had stopped crying now.]

"What would you have?" my thought process was broken as I realized that we had reached Barista. We placed our orders. None of us had the courage to look at the other in the eye; none of us knew what to speak, probably none of us wanted to face it. After a full fifteen minutes the silence was broken. "Satyam, you are the only person who understands me. This is the most important relationship in my life. Though

I don't know what this exactly is but whenever I feel something which I can only share with my mother and she fails to understand me, it is you whom I look up to. Whenever I fail to share something with my father, it is you with whom I can share that. Whenever I want to feel loved, it is you whom I think of. Whenever I want to feel being cared for, it is you who take the best care of me. Whenever I feel I need to share anything with anybody in this world and I can not do it I know it is you to whom I can return anytime and every time. You are much more than a friend to me. Sometimes I take you as my friend, sometimes as lover, sometimes as my father, sometimes as my brother and I don't want to lose all these relations just for the sake of one. Please remain what you are to me. Please do not change a bit," she said as tears rolled down her cheek. Before I could say anything I heard someone calling my name. It was Avash. Unable to find us in college he had guessed we would be at Barista.

4

"Hey! How are you guys doing? You know what? I am just coming from Career Launchers. A new weekend batch is starting tomorrow and they are willing to offer 20% discount if we join now. Let us do it man," Avash said in one breath. Avash wanted to do an MBA. One of the positives of being born in a highly educated family is that all your career aspirations and goals are already laid out before you are mature enough to understand what they mean. Not only that, these goals are repeated so many times to you that by the time you grow up you start relating to these looking at them as your own, without ever realizing that you are actually living someone's else dream. Avash had that luxury, I did not. Coming from a small town business class family I always had my father's business to fall back upon. My parents never ever encouraged me or even discouraged me from doing anything, including studies. I did whatever I felt like doing, never helped my family with the business and just kept on enjoying my life, living one day at a time. After I cleared high school I took science because this was what intelligent students in Kanpur were supposed to do. After clearing Senior Secondary I took admission in Engineering because again this was what I was supposed to do. In short, I had never thought about a career, I had never set any goals for myself and I did not know what I would be doing once engineering was over. Avash and Anisha however were very sure about their career aspirations. Avash wanted to join a B-School and Anisha wanted to go to States for doing her MS. "No *yaar*! I am still not sure whether I want to join MBA or not. You go ahead and join. Also it will cost a lot and I do not want to ask my parents for any money right now," I told Avash. "Shut up man, you know we always study together and forget about money, I am going to register for both of us, you pay me back later," he said as he left. I do not know if he even remembers for how many things I have to pay him back... at least I don't... It was my idea to steal the book and it was Avash who paid up for it.

Immediately after talking to Anisha I had called Avash on that fateful night. He answered in the first ring. He was awake and he knew I will call him. "Avash what have you done? Have you lost your senses or what? Why did you tell her about the book thing?" I fired. He did not answer for a long time and when he did; it was with a very heavy voice that he said, "Go to sleep Satyam. I am fine." I had never heard Avash like that; though he was not crying still I could feel the pain he was undergoing. It would have been better if he had cried. I softened my voice and said, "Avash, what was the need for all this? It has almost been a year and how it all started does not matter now." "It does Satyam, one day you will know it does," he replied slowly. "If it does, then how?" I asked. As he started speaking I could feel his pain, his voice was trembling now as he said, "Satyam I love her and one day I want to marry her. I dream of a life where the two of us live together, where we are always there for each other, where we face all our difficulties together, where we share not only our joys but also our sorrows," he paused "Do you think such a relation can survive without trust?" he paused again, for a longer period this time and then he said, "What is the basis of our relation?" he became silent and I felt that he wanted me to answer this question for him but I had no answer. After a moment he smiled with much pain as he replied to his own question, "A lie... A lie is all our relationship is based on." "Think with a cool mind Avash," I spoke very softly "it was my idea to steal the book, it was I who actually stole the book. You did not even know of it until I told you. If you are so much concerned about truth then why did you lie to Anisha. It was not your fault but mine. Why did you take the blame for it? Let us tell the complete truth to Anisha and then let her decide what is right and what is wrong." "No Satyam, It was done for me. I had the option of telling her the truth all this while but I never did. It is not your fault, not in the least; you were just trying to help me out. It was I who wanted to talk to her and not you. Moreover Anisha needs a friend right now and you are the only one who can support her now so drop the idea of telling anything to her," he replied. "Avash don't try to be God. You are a human, remain a human being. Stop this bullshit now. Tomorrow morning the first thing we are going to do is to tell Anisha everything and you are not going to stop me," I said rather forcefully. "It is not only Anisha who needs a friend," he said with great difficulty and then after a long pause he continued "I need a friend too. If you tell her anything, I will always feel guilty towards you and would never be able to talk to you again. I will lose you as well. Rest it is your call." He disconnected.

5

"You have still not given me an answer Satyam. Tell me will you please remain the same for me? I don't want to lose you..." she asked again. "Anisha do you remember the time we had first come to Barista?," I started speaking, "Nothing much has changed since then, we always occupy the same stupid table, order the same stupid stuff, talk the same stupid nonsense and then leave back to our stupid lives; nothing much changes, isn't it so?" She remained quite. I continued, "Look at that security guard. Day after day, he keeps standing at that stupid gate with his stupid smile, does not matter whether he is happy or not, does not matter if he wants to laugh or cry but he has to maintain his stupid smile and open the door for us whenever we walk-in or walk-out. That is all he has been doing and that is all he will ever do."

None of us spoke for a few moments and then she finally asked, "What is the point?" I leaned across the table; took both her hands into my left hand and cupped them with my right hand, looked straight into her eyes and asked, "Do you love Avash?" I was still holding her hands but not her gaze, instead of replying she lowered her face and started looking at the empty coffee cup. I did not say anything. After about a minute or so I spoke, "Baby, look at me. You say I am your best friend, right?" Slowly she raised her head and looked at me. Her eyes were wet. Instead of replying she just blinked her eyelids. I gently pressed her hands and asked again, "Baby you know Avash loves you like anything and he is probably the best guy you will ever get. Would not you share your feelings with me? Tell me do you love him?" Tears rolled down her cheeks as she slowly moved her head sideways. "Baby if it is not for Avash then why is it that you are turning me down?" very slowly I spoke. She was crying when she said, "Satyam, I will never marry." I left her hands and took her face into my hands, looked into her eyes and said, "Ok baby, stop crying. It is perfectly all right if you do not love me but at least do not speak such negative things. I will do whatever is fine with you dear but you have to be happy. Now stop crying, fast... fast." I wiped her tears and then leaned back in my chair. She needed some time and so I kept quiet.

I was trying to smile to make her feel comfortable but she was not looking at me. She was again looking at the empty coffee cup as if trying to read something into what was left of the coffee. She kept looking at that for a long period and then finally she spoke without looking up, without making any movements, her eyes still fixed at the coffee cup, "Do you remember the first time you had come to my home?"

"Yes I do," I replied as I tried to think what she was getting at. I did not have to wait for long. "Do you remember my parents had a severe fight then?" she asked slowly still looking down. "Yes, I do. Probably that was a wrong time for me to come but then that happens in every family. It does not change anything between you and me. Or does it?" Anisha looked straight into my eyes now and said, "No it does not change anything between you and me but it does change a lot of things inside me." I stopped leaning and sat upright. "What do you mean?" I asked. She had now stopped crying and she appeared very calm now. "That was not a wrong time for you to come. In my home, every time is a wrong time. My parents can not stop fighting over things. They do not need a reason to fight, they love fighting and I have decided I am not going to go for such a life. I will remain single and I will never compromise with my happiness," she said. The moment she said that I started smiling. "Come on Anisha, don't be a kid yaar. Tell me one family where husband and wife do not fight. All this happens in my home as well dear but that does not mean I also decide not to marry. If only 10% of people start thinking like you, our population problem will be solved," I said and I started laughing. "This is not a joke Satyam. You can say it very easily because you have not been through what I have been, you do not know how it feels when you come running down from school to share your feelings with your mother only to find that it is she who needs your support, you do not know how it feels when all your friends go out with their families to enjoy and party and you sit at home praying to God for one peaceful day, one moment of happiness together, one moment with your own parents. No, after all that I have seen I can not take chances. I am happy right now and I want to remain happy always, I hate the institution of marriage and I am never going to marry I know that," she said. "Ok! I would not argue on that. There still remains a long time before any of us will marry, so let us keep that apart. I am talking about love and not marriage," I argued as I waited for her reply. This time her reply was prompt, "when I know I am not going to marry then there is no question of falling in love." "Now you are being stubborn dear, how can you be so sure of what will happen years from now? What if things might change? What if you decide about marrying later? How can you close all options right now?" before I could add anything more she replied, "Because there is no option. I know myself and I know I will not change." She said that forcefully and I knew it was going towards an argument which would not help any of us and the best thing to handle the situation was to keep silent.

After some time I asked again, "Anisha I had asked you if you remember the first time we had come to Barista?" "Yes," she replied. "And do you remember you had said the same thing then as well that you know yourself and you would not change," I asked. She kept quiet for a while; she knew what I was getting at. Finally she spoke, "But it was you who had forced me to continue talking to Avash. I had decided that I will never talk to him again but you forced me to and now please don't hold that back against me." "Dear I am not holding anything against you. I am just trying to understand your view point and make you understand mine. Ok! Let us leave that discussion, just answer my one simple question. Are you glad the way things are now or do you think you would be happier if you had stopped talking to Avash?" I asked. "Now," she said. I was not done yet. I further asked, "Do you like Avash and do you enjoy his company?" She knew she was losing the argument and had started talking in monosyllables now. "Yes," she said. "Despite the fact that he had stolen your book to gain your intimacy," I asked. This time she replied in full, "Don't play with words now. I knew I never wanted to talk to him and it was you who convinced me to otherwise and now…" "And now you are glad you are talking to him," I completed her sentence and continued, "Look dear there was a time you were sure you would never want to talk to him again but now you are happy you did." "What is the point?" she asked. "The point my dear is that nothing is constant, everything changes. Though you think you always have full control over your life and emotions but it is not like that. Though you think you can live your life by rules or principles irrespective of what is happening around you but it does not happen that way. Each day, each moment, each single second we change, we change based on what we do, we change based on what people around us do, we change based on how we act, we change based on how people react and so my dear lady you should not live your life by rules. What you thought was not possible a year ago; today, not only you know it is possible but you are glad that it happened. What if the same thing happens with your idea about marriage? What if later you do decide to marry? My whole point is that you should not be so rude with yourself," I said as I awaited her response. She started contemplating, she looked confused, it seemed like my words were having the desired effect. Finally she spoke, "You might be right, but still even if I try to think about you I can not think of you as anyone else but my best friend. It is very rare and difficult to build the type of understanding we share and I don't want to take any chances with our friendship. Please, is it too difficult for you to remain the same for me? She asked as her eyes got wet again. "Not at all dear, whatever is fine with you, I am comfortable with that. Now don't cry and be happy. We will always remain the best friends and would not discuss this again. Are you happy now?" I asked trying to comfort her. She wiped her tears and smiled back.

It was getting late. We decided to move. We walked till the bus stop. It was very unlike of us but we did not talk to each other at all. Neither of us knew what to say or do, perhaps both of us wanted to give time to each other. When we finally reached the bus stop she said, "take care of your self and do study hard for MBA, no one will be more happy than me if you make it." All I could say was, "You too take care." As she boarded the bus I started feeling very heavy. It was a strange feeling, something that I had never felt before. I felt as if there was some hollowness inside me which kept on growing as the bus started moving away. I stood there until the bus went out of sight completely.

It was around 8 PM when I reached my hostel. We had a four storey building situated next to our college campus. The hostel building was a rectangular structure with a big open quadrilateral in the centre that was used as a mini playground.

There were forty rooms on each floor running across the quad. This was my last year in room No 303, third room from stairs on the third floor. Mine was a single room, not too small but not too big either. Though the rooms were provided with a bed but I had taken that out as it took a lot of space. There was a small cupboard near the right wall next to which was my computer table. Towards the left wall there were two mattresses; one on top of other, that I used as a replacement bed. Avash was lying at the bed reading some book when I entered the room. Without saying anything to him I sat on the chair next to computer table and started looking out of the window. Apart from the door, the window on the opposite wall was the only outlet in that cage like room. The yellow paint on the wall and grey cement floor added to the banality of the already morbid surroundings.

It was pitch dark outside the window but in the distance I could see the highway with tiny lights running down in either direction. Avash knew what it meant. He stood up, came near me, placed his arm around my shoulder and started looking out of the window along with me. This was typical Avash, whenever he knew I was not feeling good he would not say anything but just stay with me making me realize that I am not alone and then he would place his arm around me as if to divert some of my pain into his own body. We kept looking out of the window without exchanging a word. It had already been an hour when I took his hand off my shoulder. Avash knew what it meant and he started to make a move. "Don't go please," I said. He kept standing by my side, little perplexed. "Can you see those moving lights?" I asked. "Yes," he replied. "Why are some of them moving fast and others slow?" Avash did not reply. He just kept looking at the highway. I continued, "Do you think the person inside that car will ever think about me? If tomorrow I die, will it affect him? Or if tomorrow he dies will it affect me... No. Probably we will never even know about other's troubles and do you know why... because we all are the centers of our own universes. What is my universe... you, Anisha, my family, a few friends and that is all. Anything happens to any one else and I am not bothered. Similarly what is his universe... sitting here at this window I see so many universes passing by this highway, trying to achieve one more thing, trying to solve one more problem, trying to reach one more destination... only to find the next problem awaiting them in face and you know what, this race will never end. Before they will ever complete all these races they will die and other universes will take their place and the cycle will continue. Avash none of us is indispensable, none of us is different... each one of us faces problems then why does it hurt only when it is your own pain... why Avash?" I said as I started crying. Avash did not say a word and he again kept his arm on my shoulder. It took me a few minutes before I calmed down. "Thank you Avash," I said. "Pack your stuff, we are moving to my place," he instructed. "No, I am comfortable here," I replied. "Stupid tomorrow is our first coaching class at Career Launcher. I have registered for both of us at the Kailash Colony center. We will go directly from my flat." "No Avash, I want to be alone today. I will come from here itself. You don't worry please," I replied. Avash thought for a while and then he left.

DISCOVERY OF ZERO

6

The coaching center was situated at first floor in a residential building which was customized to give it a commercial look. When I reached there I got to know that the class had already begun. I knocked at the door and slowly opened it; not at all prepared for what I was about to witness. As I requested for the permission to join the class a familiar voice responded in affirmative. Not only the voice but the looks were also familiar. It was Professor RG again. How can God be so cruel I wondered? He had retired last year and after those two years of his painful classes, I had to tolerate him once again now. Of all their centers on this earth this was the one he had to join? This was the one I had to join? There were around forty chairs in that room which could barely contain twenty-five. Prof RG indicated at the only vacant chair and I took my place there.

God, in fact was not that cruel. Sitting next to me was an epitome of beauty. I had never seen such a beautiful person in my whole life. She had a cherubic face, was extremely fair and unbelievably slim. If I held both my hands together, they would encircle her waist completely. She had looks of an angel and big, beautiful eyes. If anything was lacking it was only her height, she looked around 5' or 5' 1" but given her petite frame even that was perfect. For a moment I forgot I was in the coaching class but then there was a villain here again to force me back into reality.

"Yes, late comer, you answer my question," Prof RG said. I looked at him blankly as he awaited an answer. "Can you please repeat the question?" I asked. I knew what it meant. I would be thrown out of the class like it always happened in college. To my surprise he did not do that. Rather he smiled and asked, "Why do you want to do an MBA?" I was shocked. In my entire 2 years of his painful sessions he had never smiled but today he was not only smiling but also tolerating all the nonsense he otherwise would never. I guess this was because he was now teaching in a private institution. I kept staring at him in amazement as he asked, "What is your good name?" I had completed three years in engineering, had attended his classes for two years and during all that while he never bothered to ask my name. "Satyam Sir," I replied. "Satyam Sir or Satyam," he shot back instantly as the entire class rolled into laughter. I don't think there was anything funny about it but in all the classes I have ever attended whether in school or college it was a custom to laugh at the poorest of poor joke your teacher makes. Probably that is expected to secure you some extra marks; now if that was true even for MBA entrance exams, I did not know. "Satyam," I replied. "Good, never address me as Sir. My name is Romesh Ganguly. Call me RG," he said. It was strange that even after teaching me for two years he did not recognize me or may be he did not want to pretend in front of other students that he knew me. Whatever it may be it did not matter to me. He again asked, "Tell me Satyam why do you want to do MBA?" I had no reply to his question. I had never thought about that. I told honestly, "I don't know sir......... sorry RG." He smiled as he said, "Don't worry if you don't know but try to find it out. Mark my words, unless you know which way you are going, you will never reach the destination irrespective of how much you travel. The biggest challenge in front of all of you is not to crack the exam but to give yourself a reason to crack the exam. Believe me all of you have the capability to achieve your goals, but those who know the reason behind their goals will achieve them sooner." For the entire duration of class, RG kept lecturing instead of teaching a single topic.

As the class got over and everybody started to leave I followed the angel. I followed her quietly till she took an auto. She had taken an auto to Okhla. For the time being this was all I wanted to know. I walked back towards the coaching center. Avash was standing outside the gate, "What happened, my dear Romeo? *Dil ki batti jali?*" He commented. I smiled back as we started walking towards his flat. "Don't you think RG has changed a lot?" I started the conversation. "Its money honey," he replied. "But still, RG is RG. You can not expect him to change. Isn't it?" I asked. "May be," he replied and then added, "Now can we get back to the topic?" "What topic?" I tried to act innocent but then Avash knew me well. "So Romeo, what is Juliet's name?" he asked. "What yaar, you will cook up anything man. I just found her beautiful, that's it. You know I hate emotional stuff," I replied. "Anyway leave it, tell me what had happened yesterday? Why were you so upset?" he inquired. There was no way I was going to share anything with him. It would hurt him a lot. "Forget about it man, yesterday is gone. You know I live in present. There are better things to do then think about yesterday," I started smiling the moment I said that but then Avash knew I was hiding something. He asked, "And what are those better things that we can do?" "For example finding my Juliet's address," I replied and I started laughing. He did not share my laugh but he did not ask any further questions either.

In evening Anisha called me. "Avash had called me. He was enquiring if you were disturbed about something?" "And what did you reply?" I asked. "What should have I replied... nothing. I told him I don't know," even she knew Avash would be hurt by knowing that. "Thank You!" I replied. She did not say anything. Both of us were quiet, the silence lasted around a minute. "How was your class? Avash told me RG is again teaching you," she said and followed it up with a brief giggle. I replied back smiling, "Yes and you know what, more important than RG, there is this girl. Oh God! She is so beautiful." Anisha cleared her throat creating a taunting sound and asked, "So who is she?" "I don't know. I have not yet talked to her," I replied. "Does not matter, talk to her tomorrow and then tell me," Anisha replied. I said, "Ok."

There was again a long silence. Though both of us were trying to act normal but none of us was being successful in that. Nevertheless, this relation was important for both of us and we knew we had to keep trying. That was all we could do. The silence lasted a few more moments when Anisha said, "all the best for tomorrow and do tell me after you talk to her. Take care of your self." "Yes," I replied, "you too take care."

7

Next day I reached the center well before the scheduled time. I did not want to be late for class again. I occupied the same seat that I had taken yesterday. Some thirty students had come by then but there was no sign of the one that mattered. There were five rows with eight chairs in each row. The chairs were stacked next to each other with a little gap between fourth and fifth chair. The gap was too small for anyone to cross without brushing against the chairs. I was sitting in the second last row, third chair from left. Chairs on my either side were unoccupied and with each passing moment my heartbeat was increasing. It was about two minutes to start when Avash came in and occupied the chair towards my right. At 10 O' Clock sharp, RG entered the class and with that my heart sank. The first topic was number systems. I was not finding this coaching thing much different from the normal college classes. In both,

I was a backbenchers. In both, I could never focus. In both, I kept waiting for the class to get over and this was precisely what I was doing when someone knocked at the door. "May I come in sir?" It was her. There was only one vacant seat in the class and it was next to me. Once again I got the lease of life, once again my heart started beating. Now I had a reason to attend the class. That day I would have started talking to her had it not been for that villain RG. "Yes, come in," he replied "and do pull a chair for your self," he added. That blind man. Could not he see there already was an empty seat? When it was me yesterday, he made me walk through that narrow space to occupy the last seat but today when it was her he would not do it. Sufficient to say that my hopes were dashed that day and nothing materialized but I made a promise to myself. I promised myself that by next week she will be my friend.

Next Saturday as I left for the coaching class, I was determined to fulfil my promise. I knew I was going to do it and indeed it proved to be the D-Day. No, not because we became friends but because that day we were asked to take a surprise D-Test, diagnostic test as they called it. I really doubt whether it was pre-planned or it was just imposed on us because of unavailability of teacher. How otherwise can one explain a D-Test just after two classes. I asked the same to center manager. The answer I was offered had too many repetitions of words like capabilities, preparation, challenge, opportunities, goal, achievement, competition etc. The reply lasted for around five minutes and in the process those words were repeated some 40-50 times. By the time it ended I was convinced that the opportunity to write that test was the best thing that ever happened to me and if I do not write that test I would never become an MBA. Somehow I was now actually looking forward to write that test.

They had provided two rooms for the purpose of test. I entered the first room. There was no invigilator and students were busy writing the test. Avash was already there; with his head down he was deeply involved in solving the test. I moved out and entered the second room. Here it was what I had been looking for. She was there in the room, engrossed in her paper. I took the seat just behind her.

I glanced through the test. There were three sections namely quantitative, reasoning and verbal ability. In all some 150 problems to be attempted in 120 minutes, around ten of which I had already lost in finding the right place to sit. Another ten I wasted in understanding the first question of quantitative section but I could not make any head or tail out of it. Being an engineer, analytic reasoning was my forte and so I shifted to reasoning section but here too history repeated itself. By this time I had started developing doubts not only about my own wisdom but also about the wisdom of the speech that the center manager had delivered a few minutes back. I always had the option to quit and I had too many reasons for that but still, her proximity was one factor that made me continue. I did some guess work in Verbal ability section and by the time I was done only one hour had passed. There still was another hour left but I had nothing to do.

I started observing other students. Everyone was engrossed in their sheet. No one was looking around. Each one of them seemed in some sort of hurry while I was feeling like the king of time. Anyway, I can never compare myself with these people chasing foolish dreams. Half of them did not know why they were there. I at least knew that. I was there for her. While everyone was busy doing Math and English, I decided to do some physics. I kept my pen on the writing pad with its tip towards her. I did some fast calculation to figure out that if I hit it with a force of around twenty newton it will land just in front of her feet. I took the shot and guess what? Same thing that always happen with students like me, miss some parameter and screw it up for yourself. By the time I realized that I had forgotten to take the angle of impact into account it was too late. Not only that, in my excitement I had overestimated the force by around four times. The pen instead of landing in front of her got a little deflected towards left, hit her knee, fell down, came back rolling and stopped just at my feet. She looked back. Somehow all my confidence was gone; I started looking down in my paper and started turning pages randomly. She kept staring at me for a few seconds and I kept turning pages. Time had slowed down and with each passing second I was feeling more embarrassed. I had just one pen and that was lying at ground. I did not have courage to pick up the pen and kept on flipping through the pages. Still staring at me she moved her arm downwards. My heart beat shot up. She picked up my pen, handed it to me and said, "You will need this to mark your answers." I could not say anything. Her face was as emotionless as her voice. I could not figure out whether she was mad at me or if she was of the sporty kinds. She turned back and continued solving the test.

There was a lot of time to pass and I did not know what to do. I tried to remember the encouraging words of center manager and again forced myself to solve quantitative and reasoning section. I was trying my best but still I could hardly solve any questions. It was around twenty minutes to submit the test when the attendance sheet came. It was a pleasant surprise. Just like her waist, she had tiny initials. Her name was Zero. I found that bizarre and read it twice or thrice but the letters did not change. Her name was indeed Zero. Surprising as it may seem but I instantly fell in love with that name, after all it was such a cute name. It lifted my spirits and showed me the way. Where as till now I was not able to solve any problems, suddenly I started marking answers quickly. For all the questions that had zero as an option, I knew what to mark. I was already satisfied with my achievement and moreover there were chances of a decent thrashing from Zero in retaliation to my unprovoked pen-missile attack on her. I made a wise choice. I submitted my sheet before due time and left for the hostel.

On my way back I called Anisha. The moment she answered my call I started speaking, "You know what, her name is Zero." "What Zero? Whose name? What happened to you?" she threw a volley of questions. "Now this is not fair. You yourself had told me to tell you about her and now you are saying whose name?" I asked complainingly. She replied instantly, "Cool down *yaar*! Tell me in detail please. You sound so excited." "I had told you about that girl in my batch. Her name is Zero," I told her. Her instantaneous reaction was same as mine, "What Zero... what type of name is that? Is she from Egypt?" "Don't make fun of anyone's name," I told her in a little harsh tone. She waited for some time and then said, "Ok! Ok! I am sorry. Now tell me more about her." I kept quiet. She waited for some more time and then she spoke again, this time her voice had a touch of seriousness, "I am sorry Satyam. I did not want to make fun of her name. Please forgive me." "Anisha, till how long do you think we can continue like this?" I asked. She took a deep breath and then replied with a question, "Continue like what?" "Do you think ignoring a problem will solve it?" I further asked. She did not reply. I continued without waiting for her response, "You know dear what I am talking about. We were always so comfortable with each other. Never before we ran out of topics to talk but things are changing now and unless we intervene they will keep changing for the worse." She kept quiet. I waited for her to say something; anything, but she did not speak. I softened my voice and asked her very politely, "Anisha do you really want us to go far from each other?" This time I kept waiting for her response. She was sobbing as she said "No." "Then let us do something about it baby," I spoke softly, "tell me what are you doing tomorrow." "Nothing," she replied, her voice still heavy. "Good! Then let us meet tomorrow; Ansal Plaza 11 'O Clock,"

I suggested. She asked, "But what about your coaching class?" "Forget it dear. I know my priorities and you know I don't give a damn about those classes. So no more arguments, we are meeting tomorrow. Done?" "Ok," she replied. "Now give me a smile before I disconnect," I requested and she replied back with a smile, "Bye, see you tomorrow."

8

I was glad I had fixed that meeting with Anisha. I was afraid of Zero's wrath and was looking for a reason to miss the class. It is not that I was answerable to anyone about missing the class but still I needed a justification for my self so that I do not feel bad about it. My meeting with Anisha had precisely served that purpose. I reached there at quarter past eleven. She was already there sitting at the flight of steps which went down till the raised concrete platform that was used as stage for live performances. The stage and stairs were designed as concentric circles with semi-circular arcs of shopping towers on either side of stairs.

Wearing a blue jeans and pink shirt, sitting with her arms folded over her knees and her head resting over her arms she looked like a picture of beauty and grace. I went near her but she did not notice. She was still looking down as I tapped lightly on her head and said, "Hi." She looked up and then smiled. I sat next to her. "So, you are not crying. What happened? Something different today?" I taunted her. "Shut up," she replied and fired back, "You are looking so jubilant Mr. Zero... oops, I mean Mr. Hero." This was typical Anisha, no matter what situation or mood she is in, the only thing you have to do is taunt her and she will give you a befitting reply on the spot. I could not come up with any reply. I just looked at her face. She was looking at me and had a shrewd smile on her lips. Soon the smile gave way to a hearty laughter and I too joined in. After a long time we were sharing a good laugh. We were still laughing when she rested her head on my shoulder. I stopped laughing and asked her softly, "What happened?" "Nothing," she said as she took my hand into both her hands.

With her head still resting on my shoulder she asked, "Satyam, tell me the truth. Are you happy?" "Of course sweetheart I am," I replied. She kept silent for some time and then again she asked, "Why do you love me?" I started thinking what I should reply. I did not have any single answer to that question. In fact I had never thought about that long enough to be aware of the reason for my feelings. "I don't know," I told her the truth. Perhaps she thought I was lying as she again requested, "Please Satyam, it is important for me to know." "I am telling you the truth. I have never thought about it but still if you persist then let me think about it and then I will tell you whatever comes to my mind," I replied. She did not react, neither did she reply. She was going to wait until she gets her answer. I tried to think if there was any particular incidence that made me love her or if there were any qualities in her because of which I felt attracted to her or if there was some other reason altogether because of which I loved her. Around ten minutes had passed and I was still thinking. Even for me it was a strange realization that even after thinking hard for so long I was not able to come up with one reason that could justify my love for her. "You did not reply to my question," she said. "Dear, I am trying hard to think but there is no particular reason that I can give you. I mean it did not happen in one day or at one moment and I do not know when it happened. Please understand," I replied. "Ok! Don't give me a precise answer but at least tell me whatever comes to your mind. Just think aloud and I will pick my answer myself from your thoughts," she continued, "now start speaking, please." It was not only difficult but impossible to win an argument against her. I started, "there are many reasons why I love you... for example you are the only one against whom I can never win an argument," I smiled and she pinched my arm. I smiled back and spoke further, this time I was serious, "Anisha I don't know whether the same happens with you or not but whenever I am with you I don't have to think what I should tell you and what I should not because I know whatever I say or do with others, you will never use that to judge our relation. When I am with you I don't need to pretend anything, I can be my own self. When I am with you, I find a reason to accept myself. I trust your judgment more than mine and if you accept me the way I am then that means I am not as bad as I think," I was serious this time but perhaps she thought I was saying that in a lighter vein. She raised her head and pinched me again. I ignored that and continued speaking, "When you are around I feel complete, a sense of satisfaction, a feeling of absolute calm in my heart. Somehow I know this is what makes me happy, this is what makes me complete, this is how I would want to spend rest of my life." I stopped speaking. She was not looking at me. She was quiet, her gaze fixed in space as if she was trying to see through the vast hollowness that was slowly developing around our relation. I again started speaking, this time very slowly as I did not want to disturb her thought process, "You know Anisha, in every one's life there comes a time when one starts feeling the emptiness that lies within. We are social entities. We need others to complete us, we need others to share our joys and sorrows and we need others to feel alive. Sooner or later we have to find that other who completes us, with whom we can spend our entire life, who understands us and more important than anything else, who is our friend." She was still looking up. There was no reaction on her face, no emotions but that was not a true reflection of what was going inside her. I continued, "Anisha, if ever I think of any of this, I can only think of you. I don't know if this is love or something else but this is what I feel, this is what I believe." I did not have anything more to add. I tried to take my hand out of her hands but she held it firmly. She again rested her head on my shoulder, "Satyam, if I tell you something will you try to understand me?" I replied without any delay, "Of course I will." She started speaking, "Tell me how many close friends you have, with whom you share everything?" I did not reply to her question but she kept waiting. She was determined to have an answer out of me. Finally I said, "Many, but closest are you." She smiled as she began to speak, "And how close I am? Do you really share everything with me? Do you really feel I am your alter ego? Think about it Satyam. When you say many close friends, it is essentially two only, Avash and me. Perhaps if you make more friends in girls one day you will find someone who is more compatible for you than I am. It is just a matter of time." I looked at her. She was looking at me in anticipation. I pulled my hand out of hers but she held it firmly. She raised her head as I again tried to pull my hand. She did not let it go. Finally I submitted. She spoke again, "Satyam trust me, one day we will laugh at all this. This is not love I know. Trust me baby." I did not feel like saying anything. I kept looking away from her. I was feeling pathetic but I did not want to cry in front of her. She released her grip and put her arm around my shoulder, "Ok don't think too much. At least now we both understand each other better. There are still six-seven years before any of us marries. We can decide about marriage then. At least for now lets remain the way we are. There is no point spoiling our friendship because of what may or may not happen years from now. Isn't it?" she said. I remained silent. Her smile had faded now. She was expecting a response but I was not in a state to give her any. She looked depressed as she requested, "Please be normal again. I want my friend back." I looked at her and smiled. I tapped her cheeks lightly and said, "Your friend is not going anywhere. He is with you. Come let us watch a movie." I stood up and offered her my hand. She smiled and took it. The whole day we kept on talking but we did not discuss that issue again. I believe by the end of day we had started regaining our comfort level with each other.

9

Next Saturday I got a bit late for coaching class. As I entered the class room there was quite a pandemonium there. Some people appeared very happy, many seemed upset. I realized the reason for same as I was handed my score sheet for the D-Test. My overall percentile score was 43.36 which I had guessed, was a good score. I went and occupied a seat near Avash. He was engrossed in some deep thoughts. I said hi to him. He just looked at me and smiled and then he again went back into his dream world. This was a strong enough indicator for me to realize that he had not scored well in the test. He must have been under 20 percentile I guessed. His score sheet was on his chair. I took it without his permission. His percentile score was 96.68. I was shocked to see that. "Man, you have cracked the test!" I felt exhilarated. He looked at me questioningly. "Isn't it a good score?" I asked meekly. Instead of giving me a straight and simple reply he asked me a question, "Do you know how much percentile is required to get into IIMs?" "No," I replied feeling guilty for I did not even know that. "Must be above 90," I suggested questioningly. "99," he replied in one word. "And what type of colleges do we get at slightly lower scores like say 45-50 percentile?" I asked. The look Avash gave me on hearing this can not be described in words. I felt as if I had committed the biggest crime possible by asking this question and no penalty less then capital punishment will be sufficient to avenge it. "No one in India, but in case Bangladesh starts accepting CAT scores then may be you will get some colleges at 50 percentile," he answered. This was an eye opener. I did not want to discuss the scores any more and neither did Avash.

I was unable to focus during the entire duration of class. Not that I had very good concentration in earlier sessions but the realization that I was almost at the bottom of batch made it difficult to sit through the class. As soon as the class got over I left. I came out of the building and started moving towards the auto stand. "Hi," a voice came from behind. I turned back. It was Zero. "Hi," I replied. I was already feeling bad and the last thing I needed was an argument with her. I started cursing myself. Probably it was a bad day. "How much did you score?" she started the conversation. "96.68," I replied, "and you?" I asked her. "Oh! My score is very bad, don't ask me," she said as she started walking with me. "Still tell me, whatever it is you should not be shy of it. Just accept it and improve further," I said. She looked at me and then said, "I scored only 89 percentile." I was shocked to hear that. Even she was so intelligent. I guess it was only me who scored so less. Nevertheless I told her, "You have to work hard. You know you need at least 99 percentile to get IIM calls." "I know," she said dejectedly. We had reached auto stand. "Where will you go?" I asked. "Okhla," she replied, "and you?" "New Friends Colony," I replied. "I study in Jamia Millia Islamia," I added. A mysterious smile crossed her lips. "I will give you a drop in that case. Come along. Which faculty in Jamia Millia Islamia?" she asked. "Engineering and Technology," I replied wondering where she was trying to reach. "I study in faculty of Bio Sciences," she said with a smile. "Oh! We both study in same university, that's great." It was a pleasant coincidence. It seemed like destiny had a role to play; why else then, of all the girls in my batch, would I get attracted only to her. But then destiny likes playing games. When things were going so smooth and we were breaking ice fast I got a call from Avash. "Where are you?" he asked. "I am on my way back," I replied. "At least you should have told me before you left. Come back fast," he told me. He was sounding a little disturbed. "Ok," I said, "I am coming." "Something urgent has come up. My friend just called me. I will have to rush back. Hope you do not mind?" I asked Zero. "No, not at all," she replied. "See you tomorrow," I said as I got down from the auto and headed back to the center.

Avash was sitting at the steps outside the center. RG was with him. "Sir he is Satyam, I was telling you about," Avash spoke to RG. RG looked at me and hinted me to sit down. I sat next to Avash as he continued speaking to RG, "Sir this is very important for us. We have the caliber but we need the direction. We are ready to do whatever it takes but we have to crack CAT." Instead of replying RG said, "What else." I was really surprised at why Avash was discussing all this with RG and even if he had to what was the need of making me a party to this discussion. Even if he wanted me to be there why was he again and again using 'we' and not 'I'? "Nothing else sir, just cracking CAT. Whatever may be the cost." Avash added. "Why do you want to do MBA?" he again asked. "I know my reason sir," Avash said. The conviction in his voice pre-empted any further questions from RG. RG looked at me, "what about you?" "I also know my reason sir," I tried to act smart but I guess it did not work as RG further asked, "And what is that?" I don't understand whether RG gets some sort of sadistic pleasure in seeing my pain or if he has some score to settle with me from our previous incarnations. Whatever it was I was not enjoying it. "I want to prove my potential sir," I replied. RG looked at me and then looked back at Avash, "How much time do you devote to preparation?" he asked. "Not much sir, with college on, it is difficult to devote long hours," Avash replied. "Define your priorities son. First choose one of the two, college or MBA. Otherwise there is no point of this discussion. This is the first step of whatever it takes," RG said. "Yes sir, I understand," Avash replied. "In case you need any help, just talk to me anywhere, anytime," RG said and then he left. "You heard that?" Avash asked me. Instead of replying I asked him, "Was it for this you had called me?" "Get serious *yaar*, till when you will keep playing with your life?" Avash asked. I did not understand at all what he was saying, "When did I play with my life man? It's simple; you have a reason to do MBA so you are studying, I don't so I am enjoying." "You will never listen to me. It is useless to argue with you," he said giving up. "Then why do you argue with me?" I asked. "You are a hopeless case," he said. I smiled. He smiled back and said, "Come with me, let us study today. You can go back to hostel tomorrow." Though not as strong enough as Avash's reason but even I had a reason to study. Zero knew me as a 96 percentiler and to continue that image I had to study. "Ok," I said and we went to his flat.

Next day I kept waiting for the class to get over. As soon as it was over I came out and started waiting for Zero to come out. "Hi Zero," I said as she came down. "Hi what?" she asked. "Hi Zero," I said hesitatingly. She burst into laughter. I did not know why she was laughing and started feeling embarrassed. She was still laughing as she asked, "Who told you my name is Zero?" I wondered for a few seconds whether to tell her or not but then I did not have any satisfactory answer so I decided to convey the truth. "I read that in the attendance sheet," I told her. "Which attendance sheet?" she asked. Now she had stopped laughing. "One that came during the D-test," I replied. "Oh, and that means you had hit me with your pen intentionally," she enquired. She looked very serious. I turned cold. I did not know what to reply. I just started preparing myself for the thrashing that was about to come. She looked into my eyes. My heart sank. "Ha Ha, I was joking. Don't be serious. I know 96 percentile *aise hi nahi aate,*" she said. Finally I felt some respite. She offered me her hand, "Hi, I am Zora, pleased to meet you Mr...." I kept looking at her, surprised at my foolishness as she again said, "Mr...." her hand still extended. "Satyam... I am Satyam," I told her as I finally shook her hand.

We boarded an auto. "Why had you gone back yesterday? You said you had some urgent work," she inquired. "Actually my friend wanted me to help him with some of the topics and I had told him that we can do that after Saturday's class but unfortunately I forgot. It was his call and that is why I went back," I replied. "It is great that you help your friends. Otherwise people have become so competitive these days they even compete with their best friends," she said. "You are absolutely correct," I replied. I started feeling as if I was on cloud nine. "So can you teach me as well?" she asked. Immediately I felt as if someone had punctured that cloud and now I was falling freely through the nine clouds onto the earth. "But what will I teach you, I hardly know much." I tried to save myself. "Don't be so modest. You are a 96 percentiler and I still have a long way to go before I can even dream of coming near you. All I am asking you for is 1-2 hrs. a week," she said. "But where will we study? I stay in boys' hostel," I tried once more to dissuade her from the idea that would prove suicidal for me in the long run. "Don't worry, that is my problem. I will figure it out," she said. I had run out of options. "Ok," I said. "So next Saturday, after the class, final?" she asked. "No let us make it on Sunday. Saturday I have already committed to my friend," I said. "Fine with me," she said. "And do one more thing. Pass on your problems to me by

Saturday so that I can work them once myself before we do them on Sunday," I requested. "Ok," she said. "That's my hostel. I will get down here," I told her as I left the auto.

It was a strange feeling. I did not really understand what was happening. On the one hand I was afraid of her reaction once she gets to know about my actual percentile, on the other I was exhilarated over the way things were progressing. It was much smoother than what I had imagined. It felt as if for the first time in my life destiny was on my side. Without much attempts on my behalf things were happening that were taking me close to her. At one point I felt afraid as I knew I loved Anisha but then I knew there is a world of difference between love and infatuation. My feelings towards Zora were just of attraction and more than anything else it was acting as a detraction for me that helped me in keeping away from thinking about Anisha. It helped me in subduing my pain and it was necessary for me to keep myself busy. Moreover who knows we would become best of friends over time. After all, this time it was happening by destiny's design and not by my plan. Day in and day out I kept on thinking such thoughts. I would argue with myself and then provide a counter argument too. However one thing that constantly worried me time and again was what if she gets to know that I am not as competent as her.

10

Next Saturday, I intentionally came late. There was an unoccupied chair next to her but I went and sat next to Avash. After the class was over she came to me, "Hi, you remember your promise, right?" she asked. "Yes, have you brought your problems?" I asked. "Here they are," she said as she handed a note book to me. I escorted her till the auto stand and then went back to coaching center. Avash was waiting for me outside the building as I had told him that we should study together on Saturdays. "So finally, something cooking between you two," he asked as soon as I came near him. I smiled. "And what was that problems stuff and promise thing? So this is the reason we should study together on Saturdays so that you can get her problems solved and impress her later," he added. "You are a genius man," I replied as I started laughing. "No asshole, you are a genius and one day this will prove to be your bane," he commented and he also started laughing.

After Sunday's class, I left with Zora. "So where are we heading?" I asked. "My place of course, though I am not allowed in boys' hostel but you are allowed in my room," she replied. "Will your parents be comfortable with it?" I asked. She smiled and then added, "I live alone." I sat quietly. This was the first time I was going to a girl's room alone. I was not at all prepared for that. I started feeling nervous. The auto went into Zakir Nagar. It went through a crisscross of small lanes and finally halted at a dead end. Left to myself, I could never find that place. As she stepped out of the auto she instructed me not to talk to anyone and follow her quietly. I followed her as she entered into the building. One glance at the building and one could easily make out that whenever it was last painted, which must be at least ten years ago, it was painted white. Black and green patches had appeared all over the building's outer structure. The façade of building was inspired by Mughal architecture. Not only the facade but interiors as well, how else can one explain the absence of any elevator in a seven storey structure.

I kept following Zora quietly as I was instructed. Finally she stopped at sixth floor, unlocked her room and hinted me to come in. I followed. Now I knew how she managed to maintain that figure. Six flight of steps, daily. As I entered her room I could not believe my eyes. Contrary to the exteriors of the building, the interiors were managed pretty well. It was not a room but a big hall, with all the amenities for day to day operations. With a television set, refrigerator, sofa set, bed and modular kitchen it looked like a studio apartment. The floor was covered with a violet carpet which matched beautifully with the light purple tinge that adored the walls. "What is this?" I asked her as she closed the door behind me, "You had said room. Is this what you call a room?" She smiled, "Whatever you call it, room or home or apartment, this is where I live in. Do you like it?" "Like it... I love it, how much rent you pay for this?" I asked. "Nothing, this is my family's home," she said. "But you had told me you live alone. Where are your parents?" I asked. "They met with an accident two years ago," she said. "I am sorry," I offered my condolences. She tried to smile but she could not. "What about your other family members?" I asked. "I told you I live alone," she replied, "come let us study now," she further added as she sat down on sofa. I followed her and repeated all the problems that I had already solved at Avash's place. Once studies were over I went straight back to my hostel. We did not talk much that day.

As I came back I was not feeling my usual self. I was feeling bad about something but I did not know what exactly it was. I took out the logical reasoning book and started solving problems. To my surprise they were not as difficult as I had thought. I kept solving them and finished an entire topic, all by myself. By the time I was done, it was already 5 AM. I went to sleep.

It was around one in noon when my slumber was broken by Avash's call. "Where have you been? Why did not you come to college?" he asked. I replied sleepily, "I was sleeping *yaar*." "Why? What were you doing in the night?" he inquired.

"I was watching movies," I replied. "Ok, leave it. Just get ready and come to Barista. We are bunking post lunch session," he said. "Coming in twenty minutes," I replied.

I took a quick shower and reached Barista. Anisha and Avash had already placed orders for all of us. "So man, how many movies you saw yesterday," Avash asked as soon as I occupied my seat. "Three," I replied. "Satyam, it is high time we should get serious about our studies. Competition is tough. If we do not give our best then there is no use of this coaching or anything," he said. I took a sandwich and started devouring it, "This sandwich tastes awesome," I said. Anisha snatched the sandwich from my hand and said angrily, "Be serious Satyam and listen to Avash or this will be the last awesome sandwich you will ever have." I made a serious face and said in a submissive voice while still looking at the sandwich, "I have not eaten anything since yesterday night." Avash started laughing as Anisha handed the sandwich back to me, "accha mere baap, kha isko." The way she said that all three of us started laughing. I took my sandwich back and added, "Ok, say whatever you have to say. I promise I will be serious this time." "We are planning to bunk college for two months," Avash said. "Bullshit! Have you gone crazy?" I reacted instantly. It was my honest reaction and this was what I thought about the idea. "And what about all the lab work and assignments and class tests," I asked. "Well at some point of time we have to set our priorities," Avash replied. "Don't tell me you have met RG again," I could figure out the words were not his. "Yes I did," Avash replied. "And what about attendance?" I questioned them. "Medical," Anisha answered.

"Anisha, don't tell me that you are also part of this madness." "I have to study for GRE exam and this is a good idea," she replied. I sat quietly. There was no point in arguing. They both were at least as headstrong as me, if not more. Anisha spoke this time, "Satyam listen to me. You also start focusing on CAT now. There is nothing much taught in college anyway. Focus on your priorities." "MBA is not my priority," I replied rudely. "There are things important than a degree in ones life. I just hope you people understand that one day," I said as I looked her in the eyes. She started looking down. "Whatever you people have to do, you do. I will do what I want to do," I added. "As you wish," Avash replied.

II

Without Avash and Anisha college was not much fun. Even when they were there I found it difficult to concentrate in classes and now when they were not with me I was finding it increasingly difficult just to sit through the entire duration of lectures. All this concept of university education, classes and lectures, somehow this was not my idea of studying. My idea of studying was to identify the topics I like, get some good books on the same and read them thoroughly until I enjoy the process, irrespective of whether the topics were included in curriculum or not. With years of hard experience I had figured out that if I continue doing the same and top it up with an overnight study before the examination day, it would be sufficient to pass the exams with average marks and that was all I was looking for.

Earlier, I lacked any reason to study but with my Sunday sessions with Zora, now I had one. I started taking coaching material to classes. I would occupy the remotest possible seat and force myself to concentrate on the topics. Sometimes I would be able to study but more often than not I would start missing Avash and Anisha. I would miss Anisha much more than I would miss Avash but I would not call her for I did not want her to know that I was weak, rather I would try to think about Zora and force my self to study for the Sunday session. More than study, I wanted to know about her. How she was managing without a family, who took care of her needs, how she managed her finances... all that and much more. She had become an enigma to me.

Saturday came and passed through; Zora did not come to the class. She missed the class on Sunday as well. Such was my luck. Whole week I had waited for Sunday. Defying all my principles and beliefs, I was actually studying hard and she chooses to miss the class. This is the typical problem with beautiful girls. They will commit something and then forget about it altogether. And we sincere guys; we will keep on trying our best to keep up to the commitment as if it was a matter of life and death. However there was nothing much I could do. Even after being at her place with her I did not even remember to ask for her phone number. This was a crime and so it was just that I should undergo a weeklong punishment.

Without Avash and Anisha college was actually becoming a punishment but like all dark nights, this phase would also be followed by light. I kept counting days as I forced myself not to think of Anisha but I was not being much successful in that. Very slowly the week passed by. This was the second week in a row when I had not talked to Anisha. I do not know what she was thinking or doing. I also had no idea as to why she had not called me for so long but whatever be the reason I was sure that I would not be the first one to call. What did she think of herself? One fine day she will tell me that she will not come to college for two months and I will not react? She might think that I can not live without talking to her but I can and this was the time to tell her loud and clear that I can. Anyway Zora was much more attractive and beautiful than her.

Next Saturday, yet again Zora did not come to the class. When she missed the class on Sunday as well I decided to pay her a visit. After the class I headed straight for her house. I still remembered her instructions, 'don't talk to anyone. Just keep following me.' I entered the building quietly and started climbing the stairs. There was no door bell at the gate. I knocked slowly. No one responded. I again knocked at the door but again no one answered. I pushed the door, a little hard this time. The door was open. There was an eerie silence in the house. I called her name but there was no response. I shut the door behind me and again called her name but again there was no response. I decided to leave. I turned back and opened the door. Zora was standing at the gate. She did not react. Neither did she say anything. She just kept looking at me questioningly. By the look on her face I could gauge that she had not expected me to be inside her house and open the door for her. I kept standing there looking at her. She was wearing white suit and matching slippers. She looked tired.

There were prominent dark circles below her eyes. Her usual charisma was absent from her appearance. When I did not speak anything she finally asked, "What are you doing here?" There was no energy in her voice. I moved aside to make some way for her to move in. "You were missing the classes, so I came in to check if everything is fine. Otherwise also, I had a promise to keep," I replied. "What promise," she sounded puzzled. "You forgot about our Sunday sessions? Today is Sunday and so I am here" I replied. "So nice of you," she smiled, "but I would not need these classes now." "And why is that?" I asked her. She sat down on the sofa and hinted me to sit down as well. "I am suffering from hepatitis and doctor has advised me complete bed rest for one month. I can neither attend classes nor do I have any energy to study all this course material," she replied. "If the doctor advised you complete bed rest why did you step out of the house," I inquired. She smiled at me, "I had gone to buy my medicine." "But you could have asked someone else to get it for you. Your friends, your neighbours, your relatives... anyone," I argued. She decided not to answer my query. "Who cooks for you?" I further asked. She remained silent, her face blank. "Does any of your friends know about you?" I continued my questions. "Yes, my friend does come after the class to visit me," finally she spoke. "But someone must be by your side 24×7," I was wondering how was this girl managing everything in such a condition. "Don't overreact Satyam, it's just a fever," evidently she wanted to close this discussion. I ignored her hint. "What have you decided about studies?" I asked her. "I have already told you," she sounded pissed off.

"And what about your promise?" I knew she was getting irritated but I also understood that it was natural for her to feel so being sick for so many days with no one around to take care of her. "I am sorry." She raised her voice. It was no longer possible for her to hide her irritation. I managed to fake a smile, "But still, a promise is a promise." Perhaps I had prodded her way too much. Finally she reached her threshold. She almost shouted, "What promise? Did my mama keep her promise? Did my father keep his promise? No one fulfils their promise to me. Why should I keep mine?" She started crying. Tears trickled down her cheeks. She was wailing like a kid. I went to the kitchen and got some water for her. She gulped the entire glass in one sip. In the process a little amount of water spilled on her clothes and sofa. I offered her more but she refused. She was still crying but now her cries were silent. I did not speak anything.

I wanted her to cry her heart out. That would definitely make her feel better. She continued crying for some more time. I did not intervene. When she was through she wiped her tears and started looking towards the ceiling. I too followed her gaze. I could not make out if there was anything wrong with the ceiling or the fan. The fan looked like all other normal ceiling fans and was rotating at a constant speed. "Do you want me to increase the fan speed for you?" I asked. She looked at me puzzlingly for a moment and then again started looking up towards the ceiling. "Satyam, why do you think Allah took my parents away?" finally she started speaking. She was no longer crying and her voice seemed in control. I had no idea why she was asking me that question. I never

ever had an encounter with Allah, neither I was looking forward to one and so I was not the right person to answer her query. "What did your parents do for a living?" I tried to change the topic. She looked at me, "They were Doctors." "Allah must be sick. May be that is why he took them away," I guessed. I did not get any immediate response but I did get an immediate reaction. It is hard to describe that expression but it was that sort of mixed emotion you feel when you pat your dog to demonstrate your affection for him and he in turns raises his leg to show his affection for you and then you shoo him away before he is done. Her reaction made me feel definitely like that dog. She smiled from the corner of her mouth, "But now I am sick?" "That is why Allah has sent me to take care of you," I smiled back at her. She started giggling and so did I. "Thank you Satyam," she said as she stopped laughing. I acknowledged with a smile.

"Shall I cut some fruits for you? You need to get some energy. We have to start studying now," I told her. "You would not give me an option. Would you?" she asked. She was smiling now. She looked much better now than how she was looking when I had walked in. "No," I smiled. She smiled back. I got up and moved towards the refrigerator. It was filled with all kind of stuff; fruits, vegetables, meat, milk, eggs, coffee, pizza, juices and beer. There were no water bottles in the fridge. All that space was occupied by the beer cans. "There is no water in the fridge," I asked her. "Doctor has advised me not to drink cold water," she replied. "And what about pizzas and meat, what did doctor suggest about that?" I looked at her. I wanted to note her reaction but there was none. "That I brought when I was well," she replied. "How is your boyfriend?" I asked. She looked at me questioningly, "I am single." I took out a beer can from the fridge and pointed at it, "Now don't tell me this is yours." "This is mine," she replied. "How can it be? Your religion does not permit it," I argued. Her facial expression changed. Her voice firm, "I refuse to have to do any thing with the God who took my parents from me." "I am an agnostic too. Welcome to the club," I said "Would you like some beer to go with the fruits?" "No," she said. She seemed to have calmed down, "But you can help yourself if you want." "No yaar, I am a teetotaller. I had promised my parents that I will never drink," I said. I paused for a few seconds and then added, "I satisfy myself by smoking grass." She smiled, "What? You smoke grass?" "Of course not dear, that was just to bring a smile on your face," I said, "But I would not mind if you will give me company," I added. She giggled, "No I am satisfied with my beer." I kept the plate of fruits at the table in front of her and took my seat on the single seated sofa next to the couch that she had occupied. "Tell me one thing," she asked, "Why did you hit me with your pen that day? That was intentional, right?" "Not at all Zora," I said. She was smiling and looking at me. "Probably the pen could not resist hitting at such a beautiful girl," I added cautiously. She seemed delighted at the answer, "Tell me frankly Satyam, is it only me or you hit at every other girl you meet?" "No No, please don't take any hints. I am not looking for anything from you. I am just flirting in good faith. I guess you need some beer. Shall I bring you any?" I said in one breath. Perhaps I sounded worried or tensed or bizarre, I don't know how exactly I sounded but it must be funny for sure as my reaction made her laugh. "You are a bastard," she was holding her tummy and laughing hard. I did not know how to react. I did not want her to stop laughing. I had never seen any grown up laugh like that before. That unspoiled laughter, like that of a child who laughs her heart out, loud and clear, until she is satisfied, without giving a damn about what the people around might think of her. "Thanks for the compliment," I could not come up with a better reply at that time and I guess it was a good reply for it made her laugh even more. "So, what are we going to study today? I don't have any problems since I have not studied for days," she said as she stopped laughing. She had finished her plate of fruits by then. "Leave that to me," I replied.

That day we just revised a few topics. I did not want her to work hard since she was not well. While leaving I remembered to note down her cell phone number.

12

Better late than never. Though I could not make her my friend in one week but finally I did befriend her and I was glad that I could. May be I was fooling myself, may be I was not. I was still not completely out of Anisha but things were certainly improving for better. Slowly I was adjusting to the reality. Many times I thought of calling Anisha and letting her know that I am adjusting to the situation but somehow I always stopped short of calling her. I kept waiting for her to call me first and may be she was thinking the same. More than two weeks had passed in this game of who calls first and now I did not know how she would react if I call her. Also I was not very certain of myself, if I would be able to explain things clearly to her. So I decided that instead of calling I will mail her. I took out my notebook and started preparing a rough draft of the mail I would send her.

'Sometimes you know a person for five years and still you feel like strangers, sometimes you just spend five minutes with someone and you feel like you have spent a lifetime together.

Sometimes you keep on planning for the big things, giving attention to all the details, putting in months of hard-work, sacrificing all your pleasures only to realize that it was not worth the effort. Sometimes you ignore the small things because you are too busy running after the big ones and by the time you realize what you have lost, it is too late.

Relations are such small things that we ignore while chasing our big dreams. We take our relations for granted thinking once we have reached a comfort level it does not require any more rearing. Is it actually so? Relations are like trees, no matter how big the tree is if you stop watering the roots, it will keep getting weaker day after day until one day it becomes so weak that even a small gust of storm is able to uproot it.

It has been two weeks. Though I know you believe that I am madly in love with you but let me assure you that things have changed since we spoke last. You know me well, so I believe that you know I am telling the truth and I don't need to justify anything. Rest is for you to decide.'

After class was over I went to my hostel room and mailed her. Within two hours I got the reply.

O Shakespeare *ke chacha! Ye philosophy jhadna band kar* and call me. It was you and not me who reacted rudely last time. So it is for you to call. Now call as soon as you see this or I will kill you.

I dialled her number. "When did I react rudely? Why are you blaming me?" "Don't act innocent now. When we were discussing about bunking college didn't you say 'you do whatever you have to do, I will do what pleases me'," she asked. "What? Is it because of this that you have not been talking to me? I can not believe this," I realized how stupid I had been. She was already normal and unnecessarily I was cooking up so many theories in my mind. "Satyam this is not a small thing. Many times you behave rudely. Both Avash and I felt hurt that day," she replied. "But I still study with Avash on Saturdays and he never told me that," I was wondering if I had really behaved that rudely. "Do you think Avash will ever tell you if he is hurt? Satyam you need to take care, sometimes you do say things that hurt. Though we know you do not mean that but still you should try to be more careful with your words," she was talking like a teacher and I certainly was not enjoying it. "I am sorry," I said. "It's ok. Just be a bit more careful in future. Tell me what else going in life?" she tried to talk. "Same boring routine *yaar*. Nothing new as such. I will hang up now lest dinner will get over. Talk to you later," I was not feeling good after talking to her. "Ok, bye then," she disconnected.

I called up Zora, "Hi, how have you been?" She sounded sick, "Ok." "Did you study anything today?" I inquired. She replied in the same banal tone, "No *yaar*. Didn't feel like studying." "So, what all did you do whole day?" I knew what her answer would be but I still asked. "Nothing pertinent; just kept lying down," she replied. "I will be coming tomorrow morning. We will be studying together," I told her instead of asking her. "But don't you have your college tomorrow?" she was concerned about me missing my classes. "I have but I need to devote more time to studies. I have decided to take a month off from college and focus on preparations. I will take a medical leave I guess," I told her. "Are you sure this is the right thing to do?" she re-confirmed. "Yes I am. See you tomorrow."

Zora and I started studying together. Though I still studied with Avash on Saturdays but rest of the week I used to be mostly at Zora's place. The month went by very fast. Zora recovered completely and in the process we became good friends. However I still did not know much about her past. Though I did ask her once or twice but I always found her reluctant to talk about her past. The only thing I got to know was that she was the only child to her parents and they had left her enough fortune to take care of all her material needs for years to come.

Soon classroom coaching sessions got over and test series started. The test series was a true test of ones mettle. Here percentile scores were calculated based on not only your center's students but across all centers in the country. Though it was still in no way anything comparable to the real exam. Avash was consistently scoring well in all the tests. He had put in a lot of efforts and it was reflecting in his results. I did touch 97 percentile once or twice but more often than not I was getting percentiles within the range of 92 to 95. Zora however was showing varying results with her scores varying from 75 to 95 percentile. Soon it was time for various B-Schools' entrance exam. I could not perform well in them and did not get any interview calls. Finally Avash realized his dream – he cracked CAT and got interview calls from all six IIMs. Zora also got calls from FMS and IIFT, both located in Delhi. This was when I actually realized what Avash meant whenever he told me to get serious in life. Only three more months of college life and, with no interview calls from B-Schools and no job at hand, for the first time I realized that this might be the end of my life in a big city and soon I may have to head back to my town and start looking after my father's business.

ONLY CONSTANT IS CHANGE

13

"What is the surprise? Please tell now," I requested as we took our seats along our favourite table. Anisha was treating us at Barista but she had not told the reason yet. "Don't be so impatient *yaar*. Place your orders first and then I will tell." "First tell the occasion. Unless we know how big the occasion is, how will we decide what to order? Right Avash," I looked at Avash. He smiled and nodded in affirmative. Finally Anisha disclosed, "I have scored 1483 in GRE." "That's great. Congratulations," Avash said. I also congratulated her. "So, which university you are finally heading too?" I asked. "Don't know which one I will get. I still have to do my research but one thing is for sure. I am going to America," she was very happy at the prospects of achieving her career goals. "What about you Avash? How did your interview go?" Anisha asked. "You mean that interviews have already started? You did not tell me Avash?" I reacted before Avash could reply. "You never asked *yaar*," Avash replied, "Ahmedabad went ok but I screwed Bangalore. Let us see. There are still four more to go." I was feeling ashamed of myself. Avash was right, I was so pre-occupied with myself that I never wondered to inquire what was going on in Avash's life. I tried to hide my feelings, "you will definitely get selected man and we all know that." "Thank you," Avash smiled, "What about you? Have you thought about what you are going to do now?" "I don't know," I replied, "may be it is time for me to bid goodbye to this city." "Shut up," Anisha said, "campus placements will start next month and you will definitely get a job." "My technical skills are not strong. I will never clear an interview I know that," I told them. "Don't worry Satyam; these interviews are not as much about technicals as you might think. More than technicals they focus on analytical skills so it will be a cakewalk for you and as far as the little bit of technical part is concerned, one month is enough to wrap that up," like always Avash was trying to comfort me even now. "Don't really know if I will be able to do it but still I will try," I said, "and let us stop this topic now. We are here to party and not to discuss boring things."

That day after the treat I kept thinking about the discussion. I did not really know if I would be able to brush up my technicals so fast but I did not have many options. The choice was made easy by the fact that I had to choose between going back to my hometown being a no one, and studying to get a job. I decided to try for the latter.

I did not feel comfortable thinking of the future. Even the present was not too good. We were spending much less time together now. Many a times I felt guilty towards Avash. He had no clue how I felt for Anisha while I was sure he was still in love with her. At times I felt it did not really matter. The kind of feelings Anisha and I used to share had nothing to do with Avash so it was not at all necessary for him to know. I myself was not sure of the type of relation that Anisha and I were sharing. I did not feel good after talking to her that day. At times I felt more inclined to talk to Zora than to Anisha. Though slowly but things were changing for sure between us. Avash did not tell me about his interviews. He knew I was spending more time with Zora than him. Anisha didn't tell me much about what was going on in her life. It might be because she was keeping busy now and we were talking less but still it could have been done if we both had tried. Life was indeed changing for me and I was not happy about it. Nevertheless there was nothing much I could do to stop this change or give it any direction. It was a part of growing up. Sooner or later college life had to end. My fault was that I realized it way too late.

14

I still remember that day, 13th day of March. Zora called me and asked me to visit her at her home. I enquired what it was for but she told me not to ask any questions and come straight to her home. I reached there. The door was unlatched. The hall was dimly lit through a candle that was alight on the table. Next to the candle were lying a cardboard box and two cans of beer. Zora was sitting at the couch looking constantly at the candle's flame. I went and sat next to her on the sofa. It was then that she noticed me. She smiled. I smiled back. The silence in the room was very comforting. The aura of peace and serenity created by the candle's flame was poignant. Both of us were enjoying that silence. It was a great feeling and I wished it could last forever.

After a few moments Zora stood up and opened the cardboard box. There was a cake inside with inscription 'Ma and Pa I Miss You'. I was speechless. This girl had seen so much in her life, but still she contained all the pain within herself. I did not know what to say. Finally I asked, "Your parent's anniversary?" She smiled. I did not know why. May be she felt that it would help her in hiding her pain from me or may be it actually helped her in reducing her pain. "Yes, they left me this day," she replied. "I am sorry," I said. She did not reply to me but she rose from the couch and sat down on the floor in front of the table. She looked at the cake,

'Ma, Pa, meet Satyam. He is my best friend. You know when I had jaundice, he was there with me. He missed his college and took care of me. He taught me as well. Today, if I will get admission into any good institute it will be because of him. You know Ma, he is not like other guys. At first even I had my doubts but after reading his letter I knew he was not like other guys. He is a gentleman Ma. I will read his letter for you,

What letter she was referring to? I had no clue. I had never written her any letter. Yes, she was a good friend. In fact I had no discomfiture in accepting that I was attracted towards her but she was definitely not my best friend. That place was for Anisha and no matter how things were between us, no one could replace her from that place ever. She was definitely confusing things. Might be she was suffering from mild Schizophrenia.

She took out one of my rough notebook that I might have left at her place. She started reading from it,

'Sometimes you know a person for five years and still you feel like strangers, sometimes you just spend five minutes with someone and you feel like you have spend a lifetime together. Sometimes you keep on planning for the big things, giving attention to all the details, putting in months of hard-work, sacrificing all your pleasures only to realize that it was not worth the effort. Sometimes you ignore the small things because you are too busy running after the big ones and by the time you realize what you have lost, it is too late.

Relationship are such small things that we ignore while chasing our big dreams. We take our relationship for granted thinking once we have reached a comfort level it does not require any more rearing. Is it actually so? Relationship are like trees, no matter how big the tree is if you stop watering the roots, it will keep getting weaker day after day until one day it becomes so week that even a small gust of storm is able to uproot it.

It has been two weeks. Though I know you believe that I am madly in love with you but let me assure you that things have changed since we spoke last. You know me well, so I believe that you know I am telling the truth and I don't need to justify anything. Rest is for you to decide.'

She looked at me. She had tears in her eyes. I was too dumbfounded to react. That letter was not for her. She was certainly mistaken. She continued talking to her parents,

'Ma, he is a true friend. He is true at heart. After a long time I have found a true friend. Everything that is dear to me, Allah takes that away. Please tell Allah not to mess up with our friendship. I wish you could be here to meet him. I miss you Ma, I miss you Pa'

She had tears rolling down her cheeks as she cut the cake and offered me a piece. I rose from the couch and sat down on the floor next to her. I took the cake from her hand and took it near her mouth. I wanted her to have a bite first. She obliged. At that moment I did not know whether I should tell her about Anisha and the letter or not. She was already too weak and I did not want to add to her misery. If this misunderstanding could make her feel good then probably it was worth it.

She opened one beer can for me and took the other herself. Though by looking at the empty cans when we studied together I could easily realize that she drank almost daily but never before had she drunk in front of me. Perhaps drinking was her way of dealing with her loss. I had been a teetotaller by choice but today I could not say no. I took the beer. We did not talk. We kept sitting next to each other and drinking the beer silently. Sometimes silence can convey much more than words possibly could. This was one of those moments. By the time beer was over Zora was feeling sleepy. I told her to go to bed and sleep but she said that she wanted to sleep on floor, near Ma and Pa. I took out the mattress from her bed and laid it down on the floor. She lay down on it. I covered her with a quilt. "Goodbye," I said. She looked at me and with her eyes wet she replied, "Thank You." I had no words to offer. I smiled at her and tapped her forehead. It was getting late. I decided to leave. As I closed the door behind me I looked at her. She was smiling. I bid her goodbye one final time and left.

15

We all were busy with our own goals. I was preparing hard for the campus placements. Avash was busy giving his IIM interviews. Anisha was busy looking for admission in States. Zora was busy preparing for her MBA interviews. Though we were not meeting very often now but still I was in touch with everyone through phone.

I sat for the campus placements and to my astonishment Avash was actually correct. The written exams consisted mostly of analytical problems. I never faced problem with those but my weak point was interviews. Even if I would crack the HR interviews I would face difficulties in facing the technical interviews. The competition was tough, as such it was difficult to get placed in highly sought after firms but the situation was not similar across the firms. I got my fair share of chances and finally I landed with offers in two IT firms, one in Bangalore and another in Noida.

Meanwhile Avash had stopped almost all outdoor activities. He was doing a lot of hard work preparing for his interviews. This was his chance. He had put in a lot of hard work to reach the interview stage. This was the last barrier he had to cross before he could realize his dream. In the end his hard work did pay off. Avash achieved what was long due to him. He got admission invitations from Ahmedabad, Bangalore and Lucknow. He decided to join IIM Ahmedabad.

During all this while though I did interact with Anisha but not as frequently as with Avash and Zora. She was working hard trying to cull out information about various US varsities and the scholarships they offered. I did not want to disturb her in any way. Though things were almost normal between us but I did not trust myself enough to take any chances lest we might fight again. Finally she realized her American dreams. She was offered admission by Texas Tech University on full scholarship.

I believe destiny should have given Zora a fair deal. She had already seen much more pain then she should have for her age. On top of that she was sick for almost a month and missed out on preparation during that period. However destiny was not fair to Zora. Despite her hard work she could not translate the interview calls into final selection. She finally took a job with some pharmaceutical firm based in Gurgaon.

Sometimes I feel Zora was right. Either Allah did not exist or in case he did, he was definitely not on Zora's side.

16

It was last day of our final exams. It meant that college was over and all of us would be going in our own different directions now. None of us knew when we would meet next. Anisha was supposed to leave for States next day. We decided to meet at our favourite haunt for what could be one last time. I called Zora as well. She was such a good friend to me now that I wanted all of us to know each other well and this was the last time that was possible.

When we reached Barista, Zora was already there waiting for us. We exchanged greetings and occupied the table next to the glass wall. "Let me introduce my friends. You have already met Avash in the coaching classes. This is Anisha. We three are like best friends, always inseparable in college. Anisha meet Zora. My friend from coaching classes," I did the formal introduction as we placed our orders.

"So have you finally decided which company to join?" Avash started the conversation. "*Yaar* both companies look similar to me. What I am really thinking is whether to go to Noida or Bangalore," I replied honestly. "That is easy to decide. Stay in Noida. That is close to Delhi," Anisha tried to sort it out for me. "For me it does not matter. Delhi is not my hometown. I have already seen Noida. May be I will now see Bangalore," I told whatever came to my mind. "But if you stay in Noida we will be able to meet more often," Zora said. "Yes, may be," I replied, "let us leave my dilemma for the time being. Let us talk about others. What about you Anisha? Everything is settled for you?" "Sort of, I have got hostel accommodation. There are many Indians in my block. I hope it will be a smooth ride," she replied and then asked Avash, "What about you Avash? When does your session start?" "I still have a month or so. I guess I will go to States to meet my parents once. Won't get a chance again for next two years," Avash was looking at Anisha as he said that. There was no reaction from her. "That is great, you people can tour US together," Zora suggested. "May be," Avash said, "what about you Zora? What are your plans like?" "No grand plans yaar. I am not as intelligent as you people. I am joining a small pharmaceutical firm in Gurgaon next month," Zora was obviously unhappy with her results. "Don't lose heart Zora. You had almost made it and it does..." I tried to solace Zora but she did not let me complete. "Yes, almost... almost..." she paused in between and then she smiled, "what about going to disc now?" "Now?" Anisha was surprised and so were we. "Yes, think of it. How good it will be to recollect these memories after years. Who knows when we will meet next. Let us celebrate our times now that we are together," Zora reasoned. "But I have a flight to catch tomorrow," Anisha was not too keen about the idea. Avash intervened, "Zora is right Anisha. Let us make this evening memorable. We will go to Elevate, that will not be far from your house and we will come out by one. What do you say Satyam?" He directed the question to me but he was looking at Anisha. "I am game," I replied. "What about you Anisha? All of us want to go," Avash now asked her directly. "Ok," she replied, "but better move now. It will take time to reach there."

I had never been to a disc before. But from the movies I had imagined it to be lively place with couples dancing to fast tunes. When I entered the real disc, I found it a bit congested than what they show in the movies. Another difference was that very few couples were on the dance floor. Most of the couples were sitting or lying on couches and were busy romancing with each other. Dance floor was mostly occupied by singles. One reason could be that a rock band was performing that day. There was little scope for intimate dancing. All you were supposed to do was to stand on the dance floor and bang your head to and fro in air irrespective of whether you understood the lyrics or not. Since everyone was doing that we also joined them.

The bad part about being in the disc was that it was full of smoke. The good part was that there were two complimentary drinks for each entry. The best was that Avash and Anisha did not drink at all and so I and Zora could get four drinks each. I had already tried beer at Zora's place and it did not have any effect on me. I knew I was internally too strong to get drunk. Moreover I wanted this night to be memorable so I decided to have my share of four pegs of vodka. Zora had her four.

After some time the rock band left and DJ started playing the fast numbers. We hit the dance floor. Avash was dancing with Anisha and I was paired with Zora. I was feeling good. I did not know how to dance but somehow I was making all the right moves. I realized dancing was a cakewalk especially if you are already down four pegs. We were still enjoying when Avash and Anisha came up to us, "Time to leave guys. Let us move." "No, you people go. We want to stay we are enjoying," I replied while I continued to dance. "Guys, you both are drunk. I can not leave you like this. Come, we have to move. Anisha is getting late," Avash persisted. "You go and drop Anisha. I will drop Zora later. Don't worry I am not drunk and we can manage. You carry on," I told Avash. "Are you sure?" Avash again inquired. "Three hundred percent," I replied. Avash left with Anisha and we continued to dance till 3 AM. Finally we decided to leave. We took a cab to Zora's place.

Very quietly we entered her building. No one should know that Zora was drunk or she would be ostracized by other inmates, she had told me. We reached her house. I sat down on the couch. "I am feeling something heavy in my head," I told her. "That is alcohol," she replied, "would you like to have some coffee?" "No, I guess I will leave now," I said that but I was too tired to get up. "The cab has already left and you would not find any auto now. You are way too drunk to walk by your self. It is already 4 AM. You sleep here for an hour or two and then you can go," she suggested as she sat down next to me. "Zora tell me one thing, why do you think I am your best friend?" I guess it was the alcohol in me that was doing the talking. "Because I know you are," she said as she lay down on the same sofa resting her head into my lap. "But you are not my best friend, you are my good friend," I spoke looking at her. She was looking angelic. Her eyes were closed and she was breathing slowly. With her head resting in my lap I was experiencing a different kind of feeling. I wanted to hug her but I did not do that, instead I started running my fingers through her hair. "I know," she said sleepily, "and it is this honesty of yours that makes you my best friend." I did not hear her answer.

My thoughts were focused on her face. She was too pretty. Much more than what I had ever thought. I do not know why I did not realize that ever before. I stopped running my fingers through her hair. Rather I brought my hand around her cheek. Her cheeks were very soft. She seemed to enjoy the touch. Her eyes were still closed, her breathing increased. I slowly bent my head and rested my lips on hers. Her lips were moist. A lightning sensation entered my lips and passed through my entire body. This was the best feeling I had ever experienced. She was enjoying as much as I was. She started biting my lower lip and I was enjoying being dominated by her. Suddenly she shook her entire body and pushed me away, "What are you doing Satyam?" "I am sorry," I said as she moved away from the couch and stood in front of me. "What sorry? You thought you will get me drunk and then do anything you like. You are also like other guys Mr. Satyam. I was wrong. Now please leave," she almost shouted. "Ok Zora, I am leaving but don't get so angry right now. We both were drunk. It was my mistake. I am sorry," I said as I rose from the sofa. "Only you are in a drunken state Mr. Satyam, I am not. Now please leave," she pointed towards the door. "But at least give me a chance to explain," I pleaded. "I don't need any explanations. Never show me your face again. Now please get out of my house," she was very angry at me. I left her place without further delay.

She was too harsh to me. Even she was enjoying the kiss. I was not using her like she said. I did not know they will serve free alcohol at the disc. Even going to disc was her idea altogether. I had said I wanted to leave but she wanted me to stay. She came and kept her head in my lap. She did not stop me when I started kissing her and now suddenly she was putting all the blame on me. She was making me feel much guiltier in comparison to the fault I had committed. I don't know why she behaved that way but I was not going to let her treat me that way. If she did not need me anymore even I could do without her.

17

I reached my hostel room and sat at the window. It was already dawn. I could see the highway. Vehicles still had their headlights on. The highway was relatively free. Not many people are awake at this hour and those who are, they are in hurry. Every now and then a pair of lights would pass by on the highway. It comes from some unknown source and goes into some unknown destination. In between it touches my heart and leaves me to wonder whether this is the analogy of my life. Starting from the unknown; racing into the unknown.

My thought process was broken by the phone's ring. It was 6 AM. I wondered if it was Zora. I picked the cell with great anticipation. It was Anisha. "Did I wake you up?" she started with a question. "No," I replied. "What were you doing?" she asked. "Thinking," I replied in monosyllable.

"Thinking what?" she again asked. "Nothing," I told her. "Are you all right? Tell me what happened," she inquired again. "Nothing happened. I am fine," I was not looking for any sympathy. She kept silent for some time. "Why are you awake so late?" it was my turn to ask a question. "Avash proposed to me again," she said slowly. I was not surprised. I knew Avash still loved her and this could be his last chance. "So what did you say?" "Of course I declined, you know that Satyam," she replied. "Ok," I said, "why are you telling me this?" She took a long time to answer, "I was feeling heavy. Felt like sharing with you. But may be it was my mistake. I am sorry." I did not give her any reply. She waited for some more time, "I guess I will keep the phone down," she said when she failed to get any response from me. "Have a safe journey and do take care of your self," I replied. "You too take care of your self," she finally disconnected the call.

I kept looking at the highway. The sun had risen now. The dark period had ended and it was followed by the light but still it had no major impact on the flow of vehicles on the highway. The only impact it had was that now they were running with their lights off. They were still chasing the unknown, earlier they were doing it with their own light and now they were following someone else's light.

Anisha was going away from me. Avash was going away from me. I was guilty towards Zora. This was not how I had thought my college life would end. Suddenly every little thing was taken away from me, each relation broken into hundred pieces. I had to start all over again; I had to go for a new beginning. I plugged in my computer and started writing a mail. I had finally decided I would be joining the Bangalore firm.

SHIT HAPPENS

18

I reached Bangalore on a Sunday evening. There was a taxi waiting at the airport that took me to the guest house. All new joinees who were coming from outside Bangalore were provided with guest house accommodation for two weeks. It was not actually a guest house; rather the company had leased a few flats in a newly constructed residential apartment and they were being used to serve as guest house. I got a one BHK apartment that I was supposed to share with another joinee.

Rick arrived very late in the night. He was from Mumbai. He was thin and dark. His head was covered with a bandana. Numerous thin shoulder length plaits were hanging down from inside the bandana. By his appearance I could easily make out that he was a big fan of rock music. With the guitar case that he was carrying, all my doubts were put to rest. We exchanged greetings. It was very late in the night and both of us were tired because of the travel. We did not talk much and went to sleep. Our work life was supposed to start the next day.

The first day was scheduled for induction wherein we were supposed to get acquainted with the company's culture and its policies. The sessions were much more boring than any of the lecture sessions I had ever attended in college. Rick fell asleep after the first session. There were 5-6 other people as well in the batch of 130 who were giving company to Rick. The session was being conducted in the conference hall of a hotel. The lights were dim to ensure proper visibility of the power point slides that were being used to conduct the session. As such it was easy to sleep and get unnoticed unless you had the habit of snoring.

Post lunch almost everyone was feeling sleepy. Even the speaker did not seem to have much interest in conducting the session. Till tea break things remained lethargic but post tea break everyone was alert. This was the session everyone was waiting for. It was about salary structure and tax-planning. The session was to be conducted by some Mrs. Bharti, the CFO of the firm. People were settled after the tea break. There were little murmurs here and there. Mrs. Bharti came on the stage and spoke something but I was not able to hear her. She was not using any microphone. Section of new joinees sitting in the back rows requested her to repeat what she said. She took the microphone. She was arrogant, "I will not use the mike and I will not raise my voice. If you want to hear me you have to stop talking. If I find anyone sleeping or talking during my session I will throw that person out of this hall." She said that and left the microphone. There was pin drop silence in the hall. She was a haughty woman. I had never expected to experience such a culture in the corporate world and to experience that on the first day of job, I could not think of that even in my wildest dreams. The hall was a big structure and with more than 130 people in the hall it was stupid for a person not to use the microphone. She kept going through her presentation without any queries from anyone. This lasted till she reached the slide of Pay Package. Once she reached that slide murmurs started. Someone shouted from the new joinees, "Madam this was not the package we were offered." "Who was that... go and check your offer letter," she said. By this time I had realized that the joining bonus component was missing from the package being displayed. As far as the offer letter was concerned it did not mention any package and so the lady might as well have claimed that we all were supposed to work for free. I felt outraged at this and so did everyone else. With people talking to each other loud now, pandemonium broke out. No one had expected this from an MNC. Mrs. Bharti took the microphone. She almost shouted, "Keep quiet everyone. If you don't stop this right now I will end the session here itself." The voices died down. What was happening was not fair and I was not going to take it with my tail between my legs. I raised my hand but it was impossible for Mrs. Bharti to notice it and so I decided to stand up. I shouted, "Madam I have to ask something." Everyone turned back and started looking at me. Mrs. Bharti said, "It better be relevant." I had not thought of what I was going to say but nevertheless I started speaking, "Through out the sessions today we were again and again told about the company's policies which included honesty and integrity. Here we have a situation where something was promised to us by the company and now it is being taken away without any reason. And when we are trying to discuss the same we are being asked to keep quiet. Is this the honesty and integrity you expect us to inculcate when we work with you?" All the new joinees started clapping. Perhaps I had spoken too much. Mrs. Bharti again told everyone to maintain decorum and then she left the stage.

Murmurs started again. Many people congratulated me. A few told me that I will be fired immediately and I should pack my bags. Some told me that I did not have corporate manners and I guess they were right. After ten minutes Mrs. Bharti came again, "We will get back to you on joining bonus by this weekend. It seems like it was declared in some colleges but not in all. All the colleges where it was declared will get it. Now I don't want anyone to bring this topic again." She looked at me, "And never doubt our integrity or honesty," she stressed the last words. I smiled acknowledging her concerns but she did not respond. It was not a bad start after all.

19

When I had first come to Bangalore I had huge expectations about the kind of work I would get to do but there still was some time before those expectations could be fulfilled. Second day onwards we were put on a common training schedule. This schedule was supposed to last for four weeks by the end of which we would be allocated to different technologies and then we would undergo our technology specific training before actually working on live projects.

After two weeks Rick and I shifted to a paying guest accommodation. Though we still shared the same room but we never shared much with each other. We were different people and had different interests. He loved rock music and for me it was just noise pollution. I was outspoken and he used to speak rarely. If ever we discussed anything it was mostly about the problems or topics that we covered during the training. The good thing about us was that both of us knew our limits and we never intruded into each other's space.

It was the last week of general training when all of us were handed some bond papers to sign. It mentioned that for the next one year we would not be joining any other firm. The HR personnel said that this was the time required for the company to generate some returns on the investments they make in us. I guess they were right but why did they realize it one month after joining. This was another shock for me in less than a month. I remember someone asking about the bond period specifically during the campus presentation and the answer given at that point of time was 'We only have an emotional bond.' That answer had got huge accolades and many students had decided to join that 'firm with the human touch.' I wondered how someone can do that in the corporate world – a complete U-turn on something promised to your own employees. However I wanted to stay on my first job for at least a year and so I did not oppose the bond. I collected the bond papers. We were supposed to submit them after getting our parent's signatures within fifteen days.

Next day when we went for the training we were told the technologies that were allocated to us. I was allocated to testing department. Along with me 19 other joinees were allocated to testing department and none of us was happy about it. Though we did not know much about the exact nature of work we were supposed to do but knowing that between testing and development we were selected for testing meant that we were the unlucky ones. With the little information we had we understood that testing was a repetitive and boring process which did not require much creativity whereas development was the creative stuff that was highly respected and that had good market value.

Now I know for sure that such thinking was very premature and there are infinite possibilities in both the fields but at that point of time I felt plain unlucky. Some of us including me approached the HR requesting for a shift but we were turned down. We were told that due to logistic issues the numbers of employees allocated to different technologies were sacrosanct and we will have to work in our allocated technology for at least two years before we can request a change.

That evening I was very upset and so was Rick. Apparently Rick had one year of testing experience in some start-up firm before he shifted his job. He wanted to move to testing and he was promised the same at the time of interview but now the process seemed altogether different. I suggested that we both approach the officials together and request for a swap. He agreed. Next day we went to our HR contact point and explained the situation. She told that she would try to do something for Rick but nothing could be done for me. Instead of swapping extra space would be created for Rick.

I was disappointed at the cold way the company was treating us. Yesterday they had said that numbers were sacrosanct and today they turned back on their own word. This was not the type of culture I had imagined working in. I was much happy in my college life where though things were boring but still we were treated like humans. Here we were just another resource. We were treated like objects that could be put anywhere and then expected to do the allocated work mechanically. Our feelings, our opinions, our needs, our satisfaction did not matter at all. Since we were fresh and easily replaceable so no one cared about us. I started wondering if I had made a wrong decision by joining this firm but even if it was, it was too late to do anything about it.

20

'I am sorry. Please call me'
This was the subject of the mail Zora had written me. The mail was blank otherwise. Almost three months had passed since we had stopped talking. I had never thought she will ever talk to me again. Not only Zora, I was not in touch with Anisha as well. After she left for States she never called or mailed. I did not talk to her properly when she had called that morning. I did not even go to see her off at the airport. I had hurt her deeply. Though I was in touch with Avash but that too was only once in a week or so. The curriculum at IIM A was very hectic and he didn't get much time to talk. Amidst all this my work life was not even a fraction of what I had imagined it would be. Had Zora mailed me at some other moment I might not have replied but now I was standing at

such a juncture in my life where I had nothing to look forward to. I did not call her. I replied by mail

'What do you want?'

Within five minutes I got her reply

'You'

I did not expect such type of reply from her. I mailed her back.

'What do you mean?'

She replied

'Today is my Birth-Day. I Miss You. Please CALL'

I picked up my phone and dialled her number, "Happy Birth-Day." "Thank you," she said. Her voice was sad, "how have you been?" "Good," I replied, "what about you?" She did not reply to my question, rather she apologized, "I am sorry." "For what?" I asked. "Please don't embarrass me by asking. I am sorry. Please forgive me," she requested. "But that day you said I was trying to use you? What happened now?" I still felt bad about the words she had used that day. "I am sorry Satyam. Can't you forgive me once? It is my birthday today..." she started crying as she said that. Though I felt bad about what had happened between us but still I considered her my friend. She had already seen so much in life. Also I knew she had no close friend other than me. She must have felt lonely after I moved to Bangalore. I did not want her to cry because of me. "I will forgive you but on one condition," I told her. "I agree," she replied without knowing what the condition was. "Zora at least ask me what the condition is." "I agree to all your conditions... please come back in my life," she started wailing now. "I am there with you *yaar*. I have not gone anywhere. Why are you crying like a kid? I am with you only. I am not angry over what happened but I was angry because you called after such a long time," I tried to console her. "Tell me what birthday gift you want," I asked her. "You." she replied, "I am stupid. I don't know what I say or do at times. But you are intelligent, you should not go away. Promise me you will never go away again." Finally she had stopped weeping. "Promise dear. Now are you happy?" I asked her. "Yes," she replied. "Then let that reflect. Smile please." She smiled. "Now tell me. What have you been up to all this while? How is your job going?" I asked her. "Yes, I joined a month back. Job is cool but I miss you a lot," she replied. "Why? You must have made many new friends in your company. Right?" I wanted her to open up with people & start leading a normal life. Even after being so close to me she had not opened up with me yet. This introvert nature of her was not good and would only weaken her in the long run. She was not willing to step out of the security of her enclosed space, "No, those are professional relations & all of them are selfish. I can not trust anyone. Otherwise also when I have you as my friend why will I need anyone else?" I tried once again, "*yaar* you can not spend your entire life based on just one friendship. Unless you talk to people, unless you meet them how will you know who is good & who is bad. Getting dependent on someone is never a wise thing to do. What will you do if we fight again." She was not willing to listen, "please do not say that. My life was hell for past three months. There was no one with whom I could share my feelings. You are the only one who can understand me. I guess

I have become habitual to you. I know it is not good for me but please let us not talk about it." "Ok, as you say. Let us talk about something else then. After that we talked for around an hour. There was a lot to catch up.

21

By the end of first month our technology specific training had started. The training was outsourced to a small IT training firm. We were being trained in a tiny room which had twenty systems. So this was the logistic constraint the HR was referring to. Twenty systems for twenty trainees. That meant Rick was hoping in vain. There was no place for him to be accommodated in the batch. However after two days Rick was shifted to testing and to create space for him one girl was moved to development. This was not in agreement with what I was told. I went back to my terminal and wrote to the HR,

'Two days ago you had told me that separate space would be created for Rick and no one else would be moved to development to create space for him. Contrary to that today someone was moved out to create space for Rick.

This is the third time within a month when the company has gone back on its own words. If this is the beginning I really wonder what the end would be like.

Due to the unfortunate sequence of events that happened during the last month I am no longer looking forward to work with the firm. I am unable to feel any attachment with the company and as such if I continue to work with the firm I will only be fooling both of us.

Please consider this as my resignation.'

Within fifteen minutes of sending the mail I received a call from the HR department. They told me to leave the training firm and meet them in the corporate headquarters for the exit interview. There are many who spend years on their first job and here I was, preparing to give an exit interview within the first month of my first job.

I moved to corporate headquarters and met my HR contact point. "Tell me what are your concerns," she offered me coffee which I gladly accepted. "You had told no swap would be done but it was actually done and someone else was given a chance," I raised my concern. "See, we were finding it difficult to create extra space for Rick and so we opted for the swap. Now why that girl was given the chance, it was because she had mailed HR-VP for a change and he accepted it," she tried to explain the sequence of events. "But you are our contact point and you had told us not to write to any seniors for the change request. If she bypassed the authority she should be punished. I don't see any point in why you rewarded her," I wanted to clear everything. Leaving the firm was a big decision for me and I did not want to repent it later on. "Yes she should have contacted only me. I got to know that she had bypassed me only when I got the mail from the HR-VP. There was nothing much I could do," much more than persuading me to stay she seemed keen on defending her actions. "Did HR-VP know that there were other people as well who wanted to shift?" I asked her. "To be completely honest with you, No," she replied. "That means there was a communication gap between your team. Why should I be made to suffer for this," I was vehement. "See Satyam, it happens in the industry. You do not always get what you want. You work in testing for two years and let me assure you I will take care of it that you get shifted to development after that. Please understand that right now we can not shift you for if we do that everyone else will start demanding the same," she was very polite now but I had made up my mind and once I had decided something it was impossible for me to change. I replied in a similar polite tone, "even if I trust you and stay with the company for another two years I will keep holding a grudge against the firm. Every moment I will curse myself for staying in testing. As such I would not be able to give my hundred percent to the company. I would be unhappy and the company would be dissatisfied. So it is in best interest of the company and my own best interest that I should now move on." "Is that your final decision?" she asked one last time. "Yes," I was confident.

I LOVE YOU,
I LOVE YOU NOT

22

I knew it would be difficult for me. If I stayed in Noida I would keep on missing Anisha and Avash. That was one reason that had made me decide in favour of Bangalore. I was acting like an escapist. I wanted to run away from the truth. I had hoped things would be easier this way but destiny had other plans for me.

I called the HR department of Noida firm and told them that I was suffering from jaundice and so could not join in time. I inquired if the position was still open. Another batch was due to join them next month. They told me I could join with that batch. Finally I was going back to Noida.

Zora was very happy about my return. She had already planned what all we were going to do once we were there together. She had been as lonely during all these months as I was in Bangalore so I understood what she was going through. She came at the station carrying a bouquet of flowers. I accepted the bouquet, took out a rose from it and offered it to her. She gladly accepted. I was happy to see her after such a long time. She was as beautiful as ever. We went to her house straight. I left my luggage at her place and went out again to look for paying guest accommodation.

Unlike my previous firm this one was not offering any temporary accommodation. After finalizing everything I returned to Zora's place. It was already ten in the night. She had not had her dinner yet. She was waiting for me. By the time we were finished with dinner it was almost midnight. "Thanks for the dinner. I will leave now," I told her as I got ready to leave. "It is too late for you to go now. Spend the night here and then leave in the morning," she suggested. "No. I would not feel comfortable spending the night here. You remember what happened last time," I told her. She came near me and held my hands, "You are still angry with me. Aren't you?" "No *yaar* it is not about being angry. I just would not feel comfortable thinking of that." Still clutching my hand she pushed me towards the sofa, "Don't worry you will feel comfortable. You are not going anywhere. This is a request from your friend." She was very happy at my return and I did not want to make her sad, "I relented."

"How is Avash?" she asked as we sat down on the couch. "Why? Are you interested in him?" I smiled. "Yes I am," she teased me, "now will you please tell me about my heartthrob?" "Ok, your heartthrob is doing well and fine. I guess study pressure is very high in IIMs. We don't get to talk much now," I added teasingly, "You want his number, tell me." "Yes, why not," Zora replied, "and what about your heartthrob. How is Anisha doing?" "What do you mean? She is not my heartthrob. We are just friends," that was an instantaneous reaction. Zora was startled by my reaction, "Why are you getting serious Satyam? I was just joking. Don't take it to heart." "I am sorry," I had realized my reaction was not good, "I guess I was angry at her and so I reacted that way. We have not talked since she left for the States." "Why? Some misunderstanding between you two," She sounded concerned. "Leave it, I don't want to talk about her," I told Zora. I was upset and I knew I was not able to hide that from her. Zora had always been caring towards me. She did not prod me further.

"Would you like some beer?" she offered me a beer can. I took it. "Zora, can I ask you something," I looked at Zora. She had opened another beer can for herself, "Yes, go on." "It has only been six months and we have come so close, we spend so much time together. Still I feel we do not know each other. Why is it so?" "Because *tere ko chad gayee hai*," she commented and then started laughing. I did not enjoy her laugh, "I am serious Zora." Zora stopped laughing, "Why do you think so?" instead of giving me an answer she asked me that question as if my concern was just a figment of my imagination. "Don't you think so?" I looked into her eyes and asked her. She looked at me for some moments, "No," she replied and started gulping down her beer. She was not looking at me now. "No... then why is it that I don't know anything about your past. Your childhood... your schooling... your family... why?" I wanted to know her better. I wanted her to take out all the emotions and pain that she had been hiding inside her for years. She kept looking away from me. The aura on her face had vanished. She was smiling no more. "Is it imperative for you to know," her voice had a sad tone. "No, but I would prefer if you can share" I replied. "Can I put my head in your lap," she pleaded. I created place for her. She lay down on the couch and rested her head in my lap. She closed her eyes. I was waiting for her reply. Slowly she spoke, "Satyam, if I tell you something promise me you would not get angry with me." "Why will I get angry dear? I promise I will not. Now speak," I was happy finally she was ready to let her emotions flow. "Satyam, I love you," she said very slowly. I was shocked to hear that. I could feel her happiness on seeing me back but I never realized that she was in love with me. I wanted to put her head away from my lap but I could not do that. She still had her eyes closed. "But I do not love you," I told her. "I know that," small drops of tears rolled down from the side of her eyes. "I am sorry Zora," I was feeling bad about her. Though I was attracted towards her but that was more of a physical attraction. I did not love her, I knew that. "Please don't feel sorry. I know you don't love me but still I love you. After my parents left you are the only one who ever came so close to me. You are the only one who has always been there for me. It does not matter if you don't love me, what matters is that I love you and I will always love you until I die." "But Zora, it will only give pain to you later," I tried to make her understand because from my own experience I knew how painful one sided love could be. Moreover Zora was not as strong as I was. "Without you also life is a pain. At least this will give me hope even if it is a false hope it will give me a purpose to live for. I am not asking you to love me. I know you don't love me but still that should not stop me from having any feelings for you. Please don't ask me to kill my feelings for you. I don't have anything else to live for," she was almost crying now. "Ok, if you say so. I can not control your feelings but do remember that I do not love you. As far as our friendship is concerned; do not worry about that, rest assured that whatever we are discussing would not have any effect on our friendship," I told her. "Thank you Satyam," she sounded better now, "Satyam one last favour, please don't say no." "Tell me," I asked. "Please kiss me once. One last time," she had her eyes closed. I was taken aback by her request. I did not know whether I should have kissed her or not. For the first time I felt that even I had a conscience and my conscience told me not to kiss her but I was unable to take my eyes off her lips. They were so beautiful. Very slowly I lowered my head. I was in two minds whether to go for it or not. I reached near her lips and then stopped. I could not decide what to do. I could feel the warmth of her breaths. She opened her eyes. We kept looking into each other's eyes. She was so pristine, so good I could not spoil her by kissing her. I lowered my head and gave her a peck on her cheek.

23

My new firm was very much different from the old one. This firm indeed had a human touch. HR people here were very courteous. We were offered a choice of technologies we wanted to work on. Despite the fact that the number of new joinees in this firm was more than 200 everything was in proper order. Finally I was allocated to development. The training period here was also short. No generic training, only fifteen days of technology specific training was imparted. Once the training period got over all of us were moved to bench. That meant that we were ready to be inducted into live projects but the only catch was that we had to wait until there was a requirement for some fresher in some project. Believe me that does not happen very often. Rarely does a client want a fresher to work on its project. Whereas my training period was only fifteen days my bench period lasted around thrice that duration. Finally I got allocated to a project.

I did enjoy my work for first couple of weeks but after that it became repetitive. I was supposed to rewrite some portions of an existing software program. I had a clear set of directives that I was supposed to follow. Which lines to code, where to change and how to change; it covered everything. There was no creativity or ingenuity required on my part. Sitting in front of the dumb machines for 8-10 hours daily and doing some banal coding was not my idea of working. By now I had also realized that the situation was more or less same across the IT firms and shifting jobs would not solve the issue. This was not the life I had wished for. I needed something different but what it was I had no clue.

24

"The problem with me is that though I know what I do not want, I do not actually know what I want." We were sitting in Barista. "Then stop doing everything that you do not want. Soon you will be left only with things that you want. Isn't it so?" Zora suggested. I stared at her, "are you making fun of me?" "No," she smiled, "what I am saying is logical." "If I follow your advice Miss, very soon I would be left with nothing to do," I told her. "Good, at least you would be satisfied then and I would be able to have my coffee in peace," she said and started giggling. "Poor joke," I registered my dissent. "Ok sorry dear. Tell me what do you actually want to become in your life," she was getting serious now. "If I had known that I would not be discussing this with you. The only thing I know is that I do not want to be a software programmer and I do not want to go back to my family business," as such I was certain only on those two counts. "Why don't you try becoming a Doctor?" she was definitely in playful mood today. "Are you nuts? I am a Computer Engineer. How can I become a Doctor?" I was beginning to lose my temper. "Then my dear why don't you list down all the options that you have right now and cross out those that you don't want. At least you will have a little more clarity," she was talking sense. I picked up a paper napkin from the table and started following her advice. I never had a long term plan in my life so this exercise was painful. She was having her coffee in peace as I was busy plotting my career path.

After fifteen minutes I had much more clarity about my career goals then I had ever before. "Thank you Zora. Your exercise was indeed helpful. Finally I know what I do not want to be," I said that calmly and then yelled, "I do not want to be anything. Look at this," I tossed the paper napkin towards her. She picked it up. Everything was crossed out. She started laughing, "You are unique piece sweetheart. You should open your own firm and be your own boss. Only then you would be happy." "Indeed, you are correct. I should start my own business. You are a genius Zora. You are a genius," I repeated in exhilaration. I could not be happy being anyone's servant. I had to be my own boss. "I was joking dear. Why are you getting serious," she replied. "I am serious Zora. May be this is what I want to do," I was thrilled at the idea of starting a new firm. "But for that you will need to do an MBA and to do MBA you will have to study which you can not do so you should forget about this my dear," she still thought that I was not serious. "You are right. Come let us go and meet RG."

"RG... Who? That math faculty at Career Launcher?" she had asked too many questions in the same sentence. "Yes, come." I almost pulled her out of her chair. This was the time our coaching class used to end. If we do not waste any time, we could still make it and meet him.

By the time we reached there, the session was over. RG had just moved out of the center and was heading towards his car when we approached him, "Sir, two minutes please." He raised his spectacles and looked at me. He was trying to recall who I was. "Sir I am Avash's friend. We studied in the same batch last year," I helped him with his memory. "I know that Satyam. Tell me what it is?" perhaps his memory was sharper than mine. "Do you remember one day you had asked me my reason for doing an MBA. That day I did not have any but today I have," I spoke with conviction. He looked at me, looked at Zora and then again looked at me questioningly. "No sir no, she is not my reason. I have some other reason for doing MBA and if you want I can share that with you," all my confidence and conviction was washed down the drain by his one look. "No I don't want to know. There is a free Mock Test by T.I.M.E. tomorrow. Write that." "But sir it has been ages since I last studied. I would not remember anything," I argued. "If you do not use a pen for ages would you forget how to write?" he looked at me sternly. "No sir," I replied coyly. "Then write the test tomorrow. If you have actually found your reason then you will perform well. Otherwise do not waste my time," he said as he started to leave. "Sir, one last question," I asked him, "you work for Career Launchers why are you telling me to write T.I.M.E.'s test?" "I do not work for anyone. I work with my students," he said that and he left. "Zora I will go back now. I have to crack tomorrow's paper," I told Zora. "But what about our movie plans?" she felt dejected. "Some other time dear, Right now the priority is to prove myself. Please," I requested her. She agreed.

Results were announced next week. To my surprise I had secured 9th rank in Delhi region and 43rd rank across India. I had scored 99.47 percentile. I took a printout of the result and ran to RG. I waited for him until he came out of the center. Without saying anything I handed him the printout. He looked at it and then looked up and said, "Well done, I am sure you know your reason now." "Sir, tell me how should I prepare now," I asked him. "The way you prepared for this test," he replied. "But Sir, I did not prepare for this test at all. I just went there with determination and cracked it." "That is all you need to do. You already had your aptitude training last year; what was lacking was the right attitude which you showed in this test. You just need to work on your attitude now," he offered me a handshake and then he left.

Based on my performance in the first test, T.I.M.E. offered me a scholarship to join their test series for free. Monday to Friday I was at work, Saturday I would prepare for the test, Sunday morning I would write the test and Sunday evening I would meet Zora. My schedule was packed and I rarely got any time to get in touch with other friends. Though I did call Avash once in a while but that was mostly when I was feeling low about my preparations or when I needed some guidance with the studies. Though I was not spending as much time with Zora as she would have wanted, but she never complained about it. She never even mentioned about love or such stuff after the night when I had stayed over at her place. I was not missing Anisha now. I guess every one of us had found our peace with ourselves. Slowly all of us were adjusting to life.

25

"I am feeling anxious Zora," I was at Zora's place. "Don't worry Satyam. You have done all that was in your hands. Now just wait and trust me tomorrow you will be on cloud nine," she assured me. "What if I do not get a final call? I will have to continue for one more year in this stupid job." "Dear, I have full faith in you. You will convert at least one interview," she replied. This year I had got four calls and the final results were supposed to be out by early next morning. "With IIMs you never know," my anxiety was not showing any signs of reduction. "Come let us go to disc," Zora proposed out of the blues. "What? Tomorrow my result is going to be out and you are thinking of going to disc. Tell me from where do you get these crazy ideas," I snubbed her. "Let us go dear. Don't act like a baby. If you stay indoors you will keep on worrying. Let us go and have a bash. Otherwise also once your college starts I don't know when we will get a chance to go to a disc again," she was stubborn. "And what if I do not get selected?" I raised my concern. "Then we will go Dutch." She had said that in such an innocent tone that I could not help contain my laughter. "Ok, let us go."

Nothing much had changed in Elevate. We got our two free drinks each. This time there was no live performance. The dance floor was occupied by couples dancing to fast beats. Zora and I hit the dance floor and started enjoying. After some time the music changed to romantic notes. Zora took my hand and guided it around her waist. She kept her head on my shoulder and continued dancing. I was enjoying the intimacy as well as the music. Zora slowly raised her head from my shoulder and kissed me on my cheek. She again rested her head back on my shoulder and continued dancing. I did not react. I was enjoying it. "Let us go and sit for sometime," she said very slowly in my ear. We moved towards the couches where couples were romancing and drinking. We found some place to sit. Zora sat by my side, rested her head over my shoulders and her arms around my waist. Next to us was sitting another couple. They had their lips interlocked. Like everyone else they were busy romancing, oblivious of anyone else around them. I guess the dim lights made romancing all the more fun in these places. Zora moved her face towards mine. She was drunk. I did not want her to do anything that she might repent later. I did not know what to do in that situation. Suddenly the disco light flashed by us. "Anisha!" I exclaimed. The couple sitting next to us got up instantly. My eyes had served me right. It was

Anisha. She left immediately with that guy. "What happened?" Zora enquired. "Nothing, I think that girl who just left was Anisha," I told her. *"Kitni jaldi chad jati hai tumhe.* Anisha is in US and if she was here she would have talked to you," she consoled me. "Come, let us go back. I am not feeling comfortable here," I told Zora. Though she was still enjoying and I knew she wanted to stay but she did not counter me.

Once we had reached her place, we checked the results. I had received a final call from IIM Calcutta. I felt ecstatic. Zora hugged me and planted me with many kisses on my face. She looked much happier than I was. We decided to celebrate. She brought out two beer cans from the refrigerator. To my surprise she also took out a cake from the fridge. She had already planned this celebration. I gave her a tight hug. We had vodka in the disc and now we had topped it up with two cans of beer each. We were drunk. One thing led to other and we ended up in bed. That was the day I lost my virginity.

26

"It was not your fault. Why don't you stop blaming yourself? We both were drunk," I was arguing on the phone. "Whatever it was, we are not going to talk again," Zora told me. "Don't be a fool Zora. What has happened has happened. We can not change that now. It was not intentional. There is no point ending our friendship because of this," I was trying hard to persuade Zora to change her decision. She was the only friend I had and I did not want to lose her. "Tell me will you marry me?" she asked. "Zora I might or I might not. I don't really know. I know I am guilty towards you but would you want me to marry you just because I feel guilty?" I asked. "No, I don't want you to marry me because of guilt feeling. But is there a possibility that you might start loving me in future?" tell me the truth. "Yes, there is a possibility but I am not sure if that will happen or not," I was telling her the truth, "Zora can't you forget that incident?" "How can you even think of that Satyam? For you it might be a joke, for me it is not. Either we will remain as close as we are now or we will never talk again. We can not behave as just friends now," she had a tough decision to make. "So what have you decided?" I asked her. "That will depend on whether we have a future together or not," she replied. "I have already told you, we might or we might not. I don't know right now." "It will not happen by itself Satyam. At least tell me that you will try for it," she did love me a lot. Even after what happened she was still willing to forget everything and move forward. "Yes, I will try," I told her. "I need some time to think, I will call you back." She disconnected the phone without waiting for my reply.

I had two weeks before the college would commence. I had never been to Calcutta before but I had heard that once upon a time it was one of the most developed cities of India. Later leftists took it over. However more than the city what excited me was the thing that was Calcutta's most famous contribution to the Indian youth, 'The Bong Beauties.' Also I had heard that Calcutta was not like the other IIMs. In fact it was the chillest B-School campus across the country. Chill campus with hot bongs. That was the perfect combination for me to thrive.

Zora called me in the evening. She wanted to give this relation a chance. 'Otherwise also she had nothing to look forward to,' she had told me. I was happy with her decision. I did not want to lose my friend. We did not have much time left before I would move to Calcutta. So we made best use of all the little time we had. Eating out, parties, discos, roaming, movies, music, there was nothing that we did not do. We wanted to enjoy as much as possible before parting again.

Nature deals in paradoxes. When you are happy and you would want things to last longer, time would move really fast. When you are sad and would want the phase to change, time will slow down. We were enjoying our days together and time did move pretty fast. Finally the day came when I took my flight to Calcutta. This was going to be the beginning of a new life for me.

WELCOME TO JOKA

27

The campus was located at Joka in the outskirts of the city. I still remember the first time I saw that campus. I was out of the Calcutta airport by nine in the morning. The taxi ride to the campus took around an hour. Though it was a bumpy ride but it was very much worth the effort. Throughout that one hour long drive to campus I had not seen any greenery but once I reached the campus gate I knew things were going to be different here. 'INDIAN INSTITUTE OF MANAGEMENT CALCUTTA', was written in bold at the security gate. From outside the gate I could see the lush green trees inside the campus. I was already excited to be at that campus. As I moved in, things only kept on improving. The entire campus had a green cover that gave it a resort-like feel. Not only that, on my way to hostel I crossed two lakes. This was certainly the best that I could have hoped for.

I was allocated a room in New Hostel. The room here was much better than the one I had in the Engineering College. It was bigger, had more storage space, a wall mounted closet and a balcony that opened towards the green patch. I settled my stuff and rested for a while. It was almost noon when I decided to take a quick shower before lunch. I was about to enter the washroom when someone stopped me, "Satyam is it you?" I did not know who this guy was, "Yes, but I am sorry I cannot recall you." "It's me Rick... Bangalore... paying guest... now you remember?" it was Rick. "Rick you... what happened to your hair dude? How can you expect me to recognize a bald Rick!" He had changed a lot. His rock star look was gone and he had put on a lot of weight since I saw him last. "Which room are you in?" he asked. "309," I replied. "That means we are on the same floor. I am in 313," Rick told me. Though we were not the best of friends; we did not even keep in touch after I shifted firms, but still it felt good to know that there would be someone in the college who is not a total stranger to me. "So, do you have any friends here?" I asked him. "You are the first one I guess," he replied. "I will take a quick shower and then we can go for lunch. What do you say?" I suggested. "I will wait in my room" he agreed.

After lunch we decided to take a campus tour. Rick had come a day before me and so he was much more familiar with the places than I was. He was showing me the entire place as a tour guide would show to some foreigner. He had changed a lot since I last met him. Earlier he used to keep to himself but now he looked like genuinely interested in people and surroundings. The image that I had of Rick was of a shy guy but by the greetings he exchanged with other students during the walk I could make out that he had made a lot of friends within a single day. Though it looked surprising then but time changes a lot of things.

The campus, as it turned out, was much more beautiful than what I had perceived based on the first impression. What I had seen on my way towards the hostel was only the tip of the iceberg. It was a huge campus with scenic views and beautiful buildings that were not visible from distance due to the dense vegetation. There were seven lakes on the campus. The steel bridge on the lake connecting faculty premises with university premises looked like a mini replica of Howrah Bridge and was known by the same name. Rick told me one interesting thing 'although there are four hostels but one of them is co-ed. Girls and Boys stay together in that hostel' 'You mean on the same floors?' I had asked. 'No but in the same wing and anyone can go into anyone's room. There are no guards.' That was quite a revelation for me. After coming from a closed culture I felt happy to take breath into the open society but at the same time I felt sad at missing the field of action. 'How do we get room in that hostel,' I had asked Rick. 'It all depends on your stars. We are plain unlucky that is all I can say.' Finally we reached that hostel. That was the place to be in. The biggest lake of the campus was in front of that hostel. Over the lake there was a floating jetty. On the one side of jetty there was the lake and on the other there were balconies of girls' rooms. No wonder that was the most common hangout for students. By the end of the tour I was convinced that the campus was better than any other biodiversity reserve that I had seen, others might be greener but this one was habitable.

28

"Get ready fast. We have to go to classroom in fifteen minutes," Rick was banging on my door. I opened the door, "Dude this is 10 PM, what happened to you?" I wondered whether he was in his senses or not. "Yes I know the time; this session is by Student Council. They want to brief us about the college before our session starts tomorrow," he was in a hurry. "But there was no notice, are you sure about the session?" I did not want to go through the trouble of going to lecture hall for no reason. "Yes, there was one. The notice was put up at 9 PM," he replied. "9 PM... why so late... Are they nuts?" I was surprised hearing that. "Why are you asking me, ask them. Now get ready fast and don't forget to wear smart casuals," he told me. "Now what the hell is this smart casuals?" I had no clue about what was happening. "T-shirt with collar, jeans, sport shoes and belt," he said as he rushed towards his room, "and yes, do not forget to tuck in your T-shirt." He said that and then ran towards his room. Other students in the wing were also getting ready. Certainly if it was a prank I was not the only one who would be befooled by it. I too got ready and went to the lecture hall along with others.

The lecture hall was designed like a mini amphitheatre however it was not big enough to accommodate all of us. More than three hundred students had joined the batch. Those who could not get any chairs to sit on occupied the steps. At 10:15 P.M. sharp the doors were closed. The Chairperson of the student council came to the podium and made a welcome speech. He talked a small bit about the legacy of the institution and at large about what our role was in continuing our legacy and taking the institution to new heights. His speech was followed by loud applause. Everyone started clapping but he stopped us. "No we at IIM C do not clap, we thump," he said as he thumped the podium with his right hand. Everyone followed suit. Now I realized what that session was meant for. That was an induction session so that we could get acquainted with our culture before beginning the real journey. Finally we were going to be a part of the culture that had produced world class managers. Sitting there at that seat, thumping the desk, I could feel a sensation of thrill passing through my entire body. It was then that I realized what it meant to be a part of IIM C. I was sitting there with some of the best brains of the country. That was an honour in itself.

The Chairperson's address was followed by a brief introduction of other student council members. The way they had set up the whole process was amazing. It seemed that the entire administration, all the operations were managed by the students. For all the tentative issues that we might face during our stay on campus, there was a student representative to take care of. Once that was done we were introduced to the tutors. The tutors were essentially the students of the senior batch who had volunteered their time to help us get on track with studies. The work load in the college was very heavy. As such there was possibility of a student like me; who had not been a part of such hectic life before, not being able to cope up with the pressure. That is where the concept of student tutors fits in. This was great, seniors taking care of us and us in turn taking care of our juniors. This was what a community should be like. A community bound by the common thread, the thread of belonging to the same Alma Mater.

The induction process was planned for the entire week. It would start daily at 10 PM with one section of Student Council briefing about their roles and responsibilities. The sessions by student council members were termed as crashers. They called it crasher because their sessions more or less resembled crash courses. A lot of knowledge transfer takes place in minimal time and hence the term. These crashers were supposed to be followed by tutorial sessions by senior students. Another reason why tutorials were important was because of our varied backgrounds. There were students who had not studied Math after school and there were students who did not know ABC of accounts and also there were students who had not studied either. As such tutorials acted as a tool to bring all these students on the same page before actually attending the sessions by different professors. The administration understood the importance of the tutorials and as such twenty percent marks in each subject were allocated to the tutors. So it was as much important to attend the tutorials as it was to attend the lectures.

The induction process lasted till 2 A.M. By that time most of us were feeling sleepy. We had our lectures beginning at 8 A.M. in the morning. We walked back to our hostels feeling how lucky we were to be in such a place. Avash had told me that seniors at B-School are very cooperative but I did not know they would go out of their way to help us; sacrificing their sleep for our sake. While we were walking back to the hostel we could see that most of the seniors were still awake. It seemed like it was not 2 A.M. in the morning but 7 P.M. in the evening. May be the work pressure was actually high. When I reached the hostel, seniors there were playing a peculiar game in the quad. They were playing what seemed like volley ball but instead of using their hands they were using their legs. Though that was interesting but I had a lot of sleep to catch up. Rick decided to stay in the quad while I went back to my room.

When I reached my room and checked my cell phone there were ten miss calls. They were all from Zora. It was too late to call her. She must be asleep by now, I thought. I left her a message, 'Busy. Will talk later' and then I lay down on the bed. It was difficult to sleep. There were a lot of thoughts running through my mind. I had never given any attention to studies before. I had never been serious in my life. I never had a plan for myself. Now life had given me a second chance. Not everyone is as lucky. It was up to me whether to make best use of it or let it go down the drain. I decided I will make the best use of it. It was time to take life a little more seriously. I was feeling anxious and kept tossing and turning in bed. I could barely sleep that night.

29

By 7.30 AM I got ready for the class. I was a changed man. I was sure that now I was going to study seriously. The first lecture was of Economics. Very unlike me, I occupied the first bench. This was going to be a new beginning. Within five minutes of the starting of the lecture I dozed off. There was nothing wrong with the professor but the lack of sleep played its part. I was woken up by the loud cheers of thumping after a full one hour and thirty minutes. The first lecture of management education was over and I had got my first learning. 'Know your strengths, Always.' I got up and went back in the last row. Rick was already sleeping there. I joined suit. We were woken up after five minutes. This professor did not allow students to sleep in his class. We did not get a chance to sleep in any of the following lectures that lasted till evening. By the end of the day we were damn tired and damn sleepy.

By the time I reached hostel it was already six in the evening. We were provided with free internet at the hostels. I installed Google's chat application. Anisha was online.

It had been more than a year since we had talked last. Throughout this period she never cared to contact me. She might have thought that I was dependent on her but she was wrong. I was now completely out of her. I was not the Satyam of college days she had turned down. Now I was a successful person. I knew what I wanted to do with my life and I was very much on track. I wanted to know how she would react when she would know about me. I decided to ping her.

Hi Anisha.
Hi, how are you? Where have you been?
I am fine. Got selected into IIM C.
That is great news. Congratulations!
Thanks. What are you doing at this hour, it must be very early morning time in US.
I am in India.
So I was right. It was you in Elevate that night.
Yes.
Congrats. What does your boyfriend do?
He is not my boyfriend, he is my fiancé.
Fiancé? But you were sure you did not want to marry ever.
Yes I was, but now things have changed.
Oh, how can I forget you are foreign return... not only things, people also change once they go abroad. Does Avash know about it?
I have not talked to him since college ended.

Of course, why will you have time for us, must be hectic in States. No? Your fiancé is also from States?
I did not go to US.
What do you mean?
[Anisha is offline. Messages you send will be delivered when Anisha comes online]
Why didn't you?
[Anisha is offline. Messages you send will be delivered when Anisha comes online]

She logged off abruptly. I was sure she did not like the tone of my words. I was harsh with her but didn't I have a right to be harsh after how she behaved with me; not only with me but with Avash as well. Even if there was something urgent and she had to log off she should at least have had the courtesy of saying good bye. I was not feeling good after chatting with her. It was then that Zora called me, "someone was supposed to call me back." "I was busy," I told her. "What dear… first day of college aur *abhi se nakhre* seems like now I would need to take appointments to talk to you," she said in a lighter vein. "*Yaar* I was seriously busy," I still had that serious tone. My mind was with Anisha. There were many questions that were unanswered. "Ok Mr. busy, so how was your first day at college," she asked me. "Ok." "What just ok? You were so busy whole day. Tell me what all did you do," Zora wanted to talk but I was not really in a mood of conversation. "I did nothing; just had classes all day. What else do you expect?" I was rather rude in my reply. Zora did not like that, "I was just asking. No need to get angry at me. If you don't want to talk, tell me. I would not call you."

"Sorry dear. I was just a bit preoccupied with work. It is very hectic here," I tried to undo the damage that I had already done by my rude behaviour. "I guess I will not disturb you then. You call me whenever you get some time and please don't take too much pressure. Study hard," she told me as she disconnected the phone.

It was 7 PM. There still was an hour before dinner would be served. I decided to take a quick nap to rejuvenate myself for the induction session. The first day at college had been very tiring and it was not over yet.

30

Today's crasher was to be conducted by Placement Committee. This was the thing that made these institutes so sought after. The placement committee had eight student representatives. The entire process of placements was managed by them. One of them came up to the podium and shouted, "How many of you want to be I-Bankers?" Though all the classrooms were fitted with microphones but for some peculiar reason the gentleman preferred to exercise his vocal cords rather than using the invention of mankind that would have done the job much easily and in a much more effective manner. Almost forty percent of the students raised their hands. I would also have raised my hand had I known what I-Banking meant. "What about the others," the gentleman shouted, "you all are liars. Each one of you is here because you want to be an investment banker. Don't give me any shit about best institute or growth or education. You are here for the job. Have the guts to accept it. This institute has the history of producing best investment bankers out of India and we would continue that tradition. Now tell me how many of you want to be I-Bankers?" That person was haughty. His voice was full of arrogance. He reminded me of Mrs. Bharti but I hated him more than her because he was forcing his truth on others. Yes, most of us were there for the jobs but many were there just for the sake of brand name, then there were others who took the path of entrepreneurship every year. How could he expect everyone to be like him? His shouting did have an impact. This time around eighty percent of the hands went up but the gentleman was still not satisfied. "What about the rest? Don't you have the guts to accept it? No matter what you say, when the placement season comes all of you will apply to I-Banks. Mark my word each single one of you will apply to I-Banks," the gentleman continued to shout and talk about why we should all become I-Bankers. I prodded Rick, "what is this I-Banking stuff?" "This is the highest paying job," he replied. "That I understood but what does I-Banker do?" I was looking for clarity regarding the profession. "That I don't know," Rick replied. "Then why did you raise your hand when he asked if you want to be an I-Banker?" I was confused. "Because it is the highest paying job," he said it in such a manner as if it was the obvious conclusion. That gentleman kept on bragging about I-banking for another hour or so. Thus the placement crasher was over. There was no mention of any other jobs or streams but I-Banking. I decided one thing right then, 'come what may, I will not become an I-Banker.'

The placement crasher left many of us in bad taste. It was followed by tutorials. Three tutorials were lined back to back. In all the three tutorials we were given some assignments that would contribute towards our final grades. The tutorials lasted till 3 A.M. in the morning. As soon as I reached my room I started solving the assignments. They were difficult. By 5 A.M. I could only solve one assignment. I gave up and went to sleep. I could hardly sleep for 2 hours and then I had to wake up again and get ready for college. Now I understood how IIMs produced world class leaders. The entire schedule lasted for around a week. By the end of the week I was so sleepless and so tired that I bunked an entire day of classes and kept sleeping in my hostel room. There was no energy left in me, no expectations and no desires. I did not even have time to think whether I was happy or sad. I was not exposed to this type of gruelling before and so I was finding it difficult to cope with. To be true to myself had I known that this was what we would be supposed to do once we would be at IIMs, I would never have written the admission test in first place. There were many others who were in same shit like me. We decided to approach the student council chairperson but the question was who will bell the cat. Rick volunteered to take the lead.

We went to the Chairperson. He was very humble and quite a sensible man. We discussed our problems with him along with the student representatives for academic matters.

Many of us had started missing our regular classes because of the heavy workload. Not all of us needed tutorials in all the subjects and the compulsory assignments in all the tutorials were having a toll on us. Instead of helping us, the tutorials were actually turning out to be affecting us adversely. Rick had explained the situation very beautifully to them. They noted our concern and told us that they will get back to us after consulting with tutors. Within an hour action was taken. Attending tutorials was made optional and it was decided that instead of compulsory assignments in every tutorial session a single test would be conducted at the end of term in order to assign tutorial marks. All of us were relieved by this change. This incident was a proof of how beautifully the affairs of the institute were managed by the student council.

My first week in IIM C was coming to end on a beautiful note. We were no longer required to attend all those tutorials. As such I only needed tutorial in statistics but even that tutorial was not proving to be of much help. Both the faculty and the tutors taught assuming that all of us had already studied the subject at graduation level. Though it was a part of my Engineering curriculum but that did not necessarily mean that I had studied it then. However for the time being it was not my concern. I slept till evening on Sunday and when I woke up I decided to complete a task that was pending since long.

I visited a social networking site and created a community with the name 'I don't want to be an I-Banker' and send out invitations to many of my batch mates. A handful of them joined the community. It is a different matter altogether that around one third of those who had joined the community eventually ended up joining I-Banks. I also did not forget to send the invitation to placement committee members however all eight of them choose to stay away from it. I was almost done with it when I received a call from Zora. "Hi, how are you?" she asked. "I am doing great. How are you doing?" I was feeling relieved after a hectic week. "You had told you will call when you will get free," her tone was sad. "Yes, but I did not get any time," I told her. "The whole week I kept waiting for your phone and you did not get even five minutes to talk to me," she complained to me. I did not like the tone of her voice and told her, "See Zora I have already told you I was busy. If you do not want to trust me I cannot do anything. I have to take care of my studies first, only then can I think of anything else." "I did not mean that," she started defending herself, "all I meant was that I was missing you." "No you did not say that, all you said was that a week has passed and I did not call you. It does not matter to you how much pressure I was under, if it was even possible for me to call you or not. The only thing that matters is that I did not call you, right?" I was losing my patience. "This is not what I meant. Don't put words in my mouth. If you don't want to talk then get lost," she did not like my attitude and even her reaction did not go well with me. "Do not tell me to get lost. It was you who called me and not the other way round. You get lost," I told her and I disconnected the phone.

In the night there was a DJ party arranged in hostel quad to celebrate the completion of our first week in the campus. I was in no mood to go to the party but the music was so loud that it was impossible to sleep in the room. Having nothing else to do I decided to join the party. One advantage of the institute not being located in a dry state was that alcohol was flowing freely in the party. The scenario here was not much different from what I had experienced during initial days of college or job; few girls and numerous guys vying for their attention. People were smoking, drinking and dancing. The aura was like that of any night club with the difference being that there was no entry fee here and also there was no public display of affection. I took a beer and started enjoying the party. The party lasted till 5 A.M. Since classes would start at 8 A.M. so we could not continue parting beyond that hour. As I walked back to my room I could see Rick going to his room with a girl who was way too drunk to walk by herself. I did not know he had such a beautiful talent. The first day I had met him he did not know anyone in the campus and within a week he was walking hand-in-hands with a girl. I moved to my room and tried to catch some sleep however someone in the wing was still playing loud music. I tried sleeping but it was difficult to sleep with that music on. I moved out and followed the music. It was coming from Rick's room. I thought of knocking at the door and requesting him to turn the volume down but then I knew he was not alone. To be cautious lest I might disturb him I kept my ear at his door. I could easily make out the small voices that were not a part of the music. They were making out. I decided not to disturb them and came back to my room.

My head was spinning because of the alcohol but it was almost impossible to sleep because of the music. I called up Zora. She answered in the first ring. "Hey you did not sleep?"

I was surprised at the speed with which she had picked up the phone. "No," she was crying. "What happened? Why are you crying sweetie?" She did not reply. "Tell me sweetheart, missing your parents?" "No," she replied. "Then why are you crying?" "I am missing you," she told me. "Missing me... but why... what happened," thanks to alcohol, I had completely forgotten about the fight that we had a few hours ago. "It has been a week since we talked. You had forgotten to call me and even when I called you, you shouted at me. I do not deserve this Satyam," she was right. She did not deserve that behaviour from my side. It was my problem if I was not in a good mood. I should not have allowed that to affect her. "I am sorry," I apologized, "I was tense baby; I did not mean to hurt you. It is just that life is very hectic here and I am finding it a bit difficult to adjust. Please bear with me for some more time. I will not give you a chance to complain again." "I understand that dear and that is why I do not call you now. Even if you talk with me for five minutes I will be happy but please try not to be rude to me when we talk," her concerns were justified. "Sure sweetheart, I will not do that again," I assured her. "Thanks. I love you," she was getting back to normal now. "I know dear. I have a class at 8. I guess I will sleep now for some time. You should also take some rest. You would have to go to your office." "Ok, good night then," she said. "Not good night, good morning," I replied. She smiled and kept the phone down.

31

The first lecture was of Statistics. Yesterday's party was having a toll on us; otherwise also the subject was too boring. More than half of the class was yawning since the lecture started. The professor tolerated it for some time and then he decided to apply a tried and tested way to make everyone pay attention. He announced to conduct the first surprise quiz in that session. We were taken by surprise but then this is what surprise quizzes are meant for. The quiz consisted of ten multiple choice questions to be solved in twenty minutes. Each right answer would fetch one mark and each wrong answer would deduct one. I was quite sure that even if the faculty would have given us two hours instead of twenty minutes I would not be able to solve them. I kept fighting with the questions for some time but when the reality dawned on me that I was going to lose the battle either ways I decided to leave it to the fate. I marked the answers which seemed closest to being correct.

After the quiz I inquired with Rick, "I cannot see the girl who was with you yesterday. Is she in different section?" "She does not study here," he replied. "Oh! She must be your girl friend then." It seemed like I had overestimated his charisma last night. "No, I met her for the first time yesterday." I was wrong once again, I had not overestimated his appeal but I had grossly underestimated it. "First meeting and you people ended up in bed? How could you manage that," I was surprised and in my astonishment I had forgotten that I was not supposed to know the ending up in bed part. "How do you know we ended up in bed? She might be just a friend," he said that in a very serious tone. "Come on buddy. You can share it with me. Why would you play such a loud music then if it was not for subduing your voices," I was not going to let him off the hook easily. "You are smart dude," he said. "You bet I am," I smiled, "now will you please tell me the whole truth and nothing but the truth?" Rick smiled back, "Of course my lord, I will tell you. I had met her through a social networking website and invited her to the party. Rest of the things were taken care of by the alcohol." "How long had you interacted with her online before you invited her to the party?" I was curious to know. "Two days," he replied. If it was true it was beyond my wildest imagination, "just two days. How can someone agree for a night out after just interacting with you for two days and that too over the Internet? You are a genius man. Where are your feet? Let me touch your feet. Please impart some knowledge to me as well." Rick's smile gave way to laughter, "Of course *baccha, tera number bhi aayega.* Next time I will find someone for you." "A zillion thanks gurudev," I also started laughing.

Making tutorials optional had definitely helped in reducing some amount of pressure on us but still things were pretty hectic. The professors had started giving case studies now. So the little amount of time that we saved on attending tutorials and solving tutorial's assignments was now consumed in discussing and solving case studies. Apart from this the faculty were covering the course at a very fast pace. Our midterm exams were due in two weeks and there was a lot of syllabus yet to be covered. I was finding it difficult to allocate time among different subjects but there were students like Rick who were not only good in all the courses but also able to take time out to enjoy their life. Sometimes I doubted if he had turned an insomniac but I guess he made up for the lost sleep by sleeping during the lectures. I did try this method to get some extra time for studies but ever since I started sitting in back rows I found it almost impossible to sleep during the lectures and I did not have enough guts to sit in the front rows just for the sake of sleeping.

We got the surprise quiz marks. I had scored three in negative. I knew if things would continue to run the same way no one would be able to prevent me from failing in Statistics. I decided to allocate more time to studies in general and Statistics in particular. During all this effort of trying to balance my studies I was not able to give quality time to Zora and she had started complaining about the same.

FLIRTING IN GOOD FAITH

32

Mid term examinations would start tomorrow. It was 2 A.M. and I was still struggling with the basic concepts of Statistics. Anisha buzzed me. She wanted to talk about something but I was angry with her. Last time she had logged off without even completing the conversation. She should not have treated me that way.

How are you Satyam?
Does it matter?
Are you angry with me?
I don't know.
Satyam, please talk to me.
I am doing that.
Don't you want to know why I did not go to States.
I did ask that, but you logged off and now you get the time to tell me...where you were all this while.

Sorry.
Don't say sorry. I guess it does not matter any more... still, tell me.
Papa had cardiac arrest that morning.
What? Which morning? How is he now?
The day I was supposed to leave for States. He is no more.
I am sorry. Why didn't you tell me earlier?
I did not know what to do. I was very lonely. Didn't feel like talking to Avash, he had proposed me again then, felt like talking to you, even dialled your number many times but didn't know if you would be willing to talk.
Why wouldn't I be willing to talk Anisha? Wasn't I your best friend? You did not need to think before calling your best friend.
I am sorry. The way you had talked when I told you about Avash I felt you did not want to talk to me.
I am sorry dear ☹ I know I was rude to you but that was because of some personal issue; at least once you should have asked yaar. All this while I kept on thinking that you did not want to talk to me.
But why would I do that?
How do I know? Might be you would think that I was still after you. You were going to leave for States; you were supposed to give me your number once you reached there.
I am sorry.
I am sorry too. Let's bury the hatchet. How are you now? What have you been doing all this while?
I am not good.
Why? What happened? Anything serious?

My marriage is fixed.

That is great news. Congrats!

I don't know if I want to marry.

Why? You people are already engaged... so the next step would be to marry only, right?

No it is not that. I am not sure if I love him.

Then why did you get engaged to him? If I remember correctly you did not want to marry at all. Why did you get engaged in the first place if you were not sure about him?

I don't really know. Sometimes I feel I like him, sometimes I don't. I know no one else would understand me so I pinged you. Please help me.

But I don't know anything about you two. How can I help you? First tell me everything in detail.

Ok. He is Umesh uncle's son... you know Umesh uncle - papa's business partner. After papa left he helped a lot in managing all the affairs. If today mom is on her feet it's because of him

Ok, but do you love him?

I am confused. That is why am discussing with you.

Ok. Tell me about how you people got engaged?

Around five months back he told me that he wanted to marry me. I had told him that I did not want to marry but he persisted that we spend some time together before I decide and so we did spend some time together and I did enjoy being with him. We discussed a lot about marriage but I could never convince myself for the same.

Then how did things move forward if you were not convinced?

He talked to mom about our marriage.
What? Even without your being convinced? That is insane.
No yaar. It was not that I had told him No outright. I was confused and could not decide in either direction. He had to take a call because of his family pressure and he did discuss with me before talking to mom.
It seems like you are defending his actions. You do feel for him.
Please don't joke *yaar*. I am seriously in doubt.
What doubt yaar. Everything is clear. He loves you. You are confused whether you love him or not but you definitely do not hate him. Your mom likes him as well and he was there for you when you needed someone. You have already spent so much time with him and only after that you agreed for marriage. I guess there would not be any problems. You are unnecessarily worrying.
May be you are right. But then why am I having second thoughts... I don't know. I am really stupid, wasting your time as well. You must be busy.
Busy? For you? No dear never
Thank you. I know I could always count on you. I am feeling light already.
My pleasure ☺
Tell me what is up with you?
Nothing much. A difficult exam tomorrow, might flunk. I was trying to study when you pinged.
Oh, I am sorry. Why didn't you tell me earlier? You shouldn't be wasting your time now.

Don't worry dear. Anyway, time spend talking to you is never a waste. I always cherish that.
Me too ☺ Would not disturb you any further. You study now, will talk to you later. All the best.
Take care.
Miss you. You take care too.

33

Mid-term examination results were announced. I scored well in almost all the courses but Statistics. There were no multiple choice questions and to make things worse the marks were given only on final answer, not on intermediate steps, and that too if it was correct up to fourth decimal place. I scored two marks in the exam. My cumulative score was now minus one out of fifty.

I called Zora. "Hi Zora." "Hi, your exams got over? How did you fare?" she asked. "Got screwed in Statistics; other exams were ok," I told her. "How much did you score in Statistics?" "Two out of forty," I told her. "Oh that is bad. You must be feeling awful," she reacted generally. "You don't need to be an Einstein to figure out how I am feeling. Please don't make fun of me," I told her. "I am sorry, I did not mean that." "Oh no, I am sorry. I guess am taking a lot of tension. I am taking out my frustration on you," I knew that I was not able to give her due care since a long time. "It is alright, I can understand you are under a lot of pressure," she had no complaints with me. "Stop discussing me yaar. My life will continue to go on like this. You tell me, how have you been? How is your work going?" finally I had the courtesy to realize that even she had a life and I should bother about that as well. "Work is going good. I got promoted last week," she told me. "What? You got promoted last week and you are telling me now. Why didn't you tell me earlier?" I almost shouted at her. "You were busy with your exams. I thought I would not disturb you," she justified her stance. "This is not done Zora. As if you do not call me otherwise. You should have told me but leave it. I guess I am no more important to you," I registered my anguish with her. "Please do not speak like that. You know you are the most important individual in my life. I am sorry," she tried to appease me. "It is ok. No need to feel sorry. I guess I will keep the phone down now. Take care." "Satyam, at least congratulate me on my promotion before you keep the phone down. It will make me feel good," her voice was heavy. "Oh shit," I cursed myself mentally as I realized I had not congratulated her on her achievement, "I am sorry baby, I am very happy for you. May you get many, many more promotions. May you always be successful dear." "Thanks," she replied with a heavy voice.

Rick was banging heavily at my door. "Hold your horses man," I opened the door, "what is the matter with you?" "Do you remember the girl whom I had invited to the party?" he asked. I calmed down. Whatever was going to come; it deserved banging that door. "Yes I do," I told him. "Ready for some fun?" he gave a wicked smile. "With her," I wondered what he meant. "No asshole, she is my property. Not with her but with her friend," he was definitely a Casanova. "Sounds interesting. Don't keep standing at the gate. Walk in," I told him as I moved aside to let him in the room. "This is her chat id, just add her," he handed me a piece of paper. "But what do I tell her? She would ask from where I got her id? I was being sensible. There was no point in taking so much trouble if the result was going to be null. "That has already been taken care of. She is single and she is ready to mingle. Just tell her you are Rick's friend from IIM C. She will add you. Add her now. She is online. Happy chatting." He had guided me enough before he left. Now it was up to me to match up to his expectations.

Without wasting any time I send her a chat request. She accepted instantly. Rick was right. She was online.
Hi there. Rick told me to add you
Yes, I know
...
So?
So what?
What do you do?
I study in IIM C
That is cool
Yea. What do you do?
I am doing my graduation. I will sit for CAT this year.

Great. How is your preparation going?
Ok. But it will be great if you can give me some tips.
Anytime lady, I am always willing to help. What is your name by the way?
Jhilmil
That is a cool name. So you are like a jhilmil star ☺
That is for you to find out :P
Well, I would love to find out. Can you share your picture with me?
Why? Are you afraid I am ugly?
No, not like that but would like to know whom I am talking to.
Ok. Let us both exchange pics but you send first.
Ok.
...
You look gorgeous Jhilmil.
Really?
You have any doubts?
Are you making fun of me?
No yaar. Trust me, you look beautiful ☺
You are very handsome too ☺
Thanks !! Do you think we should meet?
May be ☺
When and where?
Let us see. Not today, mamma is at home. May be we can meet tomorrow when mamma is out.
Great ☺
Chalo, I will log off now else mamma will get to know. Talk to you later.

Ok. See you. Bye ☺

Bye ☺

    I ran straight towards Rick's room, "Man what was that? This girl was so fast. You are a genius." "*Manta hai gurudev ko?*" he replied boastfully. "Yes gurudev. *Kahan se dhoond ke late ho aise item. Jara mujhe bhi to batao apna source,*" I accepted his supremacy. "*Baccha*, eat the mangoes, don't count the trees," he smiled in his peculiarly wicked manner. "Ok. Sir, tell me what to do next. She might want to meet tomorrow. She was saying let us meet when mamma is not at home," I smiled. "Indeed she is fast. Next thing to do is to buy protection," he told me. "What do you mean," though I understood what he meant but I had not expected him to be so open about it. "What I mean is make sure you don't get AIDS," he was even more blatant now. "You mean she will go out and out in the first meeting itself," very hesitatingly I asked him. "That depends on your caliber *baccha*. Now don't waste your guru's time. He has many other girls to take care of." He started typing in the chat windows that were open on his system.

34

I had just woken up when my attention went to the laptop screen. Anisha had tried to ping me while I was asleep.
Hi. You there?
_____45 minutes
Helloooooooooooooooo, knock knock. Anyone home?
_____35 minutes
I could see she was still online. I immediately replied to her.
Hi. I was asleep.
Ok.
How have you been?
Fought with Martin ☹
Who Martin?
My fiancé. Who else.
Why did you fight?
He says we should move to Mumbai after marriage.

Why?
Obviously, because his family lives there. Why else?
So, what is the issue?
I want to stay with mama.
After marriage that is not possible dear.
I don't want to marry.
You people have fought seriously this time?
I have told him I am not going to marry him. I can not live life on his terms.
But dear you do have to make compromises when you step into married life.
That is not necessary.
Agreed. But that happens only when there is understanding between two people. You should talk to each other and not fight.
But when we talk, we fight. He does not understand me.
Do you understand him?
What do you mean?
Leave that. See it is natural for you to feel this way. Once you will get married, mama will be alone and you would not like that. Talk to him peacefully; make him understand your concerns but also try to understand his view point. This is not an issue on which you should break a relation. Talk to him and things will work out.
You are too good. You understand me so well. Why can't he be like you?
It does not matter. Don't marry him, marry me :P
Ha ha. You have not stopped your habit of flirting.
Chal abhi I have to get ready for class. Take care.

Bye ☺

I had just finished chatting with Anisha when Jhilmil buzzed me.

Hi. What is today's plan?

Nothing as such. Have some classes. You tell.

Want to meet today?

Ok. When?

At 11, my place, hope you don't have any class then.

I have, but don't worry. I will mark my attendance and come out. Tell me the address.

Give me your number. I will sms you.

9830520532

Ok. See you at 11

Sure ☺

35

At 10 'o clock I moved out of the lecture hall after marking my attendance. I had told Rick to put proxy for me in the remaining lectures for the day. Even if I got caught the only penalty would be a warning and penalty of one attendance. With the penalty being so mild this risk was worth a chance. I did remember to buy protection on my way. I reached the address fifteen minutes before time and called her. She did not answer my call. I called again. She did not respond again.

May be I was being taken for a ride. May be I will ring the bell and it will be a wrong address. May be it was just a prank. May be Rick was also involved in this prank. May be it was something dangerous. What if I go inside the house and someone kidnaps me, what if someone takes my pictures and blackmail me later. Such news was very rampant on all the Hindi news channels. I had to be extra cautious. These were days of crime and deception. There was no place in this world for civilized citizens like me.

I tried my luck one last time. This time she answered my call. "Hi, where are you?" "I am standing outside your building. Why did not you pick my call earlier?" I was suspicious. "I was getting ready for a shower. Listen I will unlatch the door. You come inside and make yourself at home. Meanwhile I will get done with my shower," she was so casual about the stuff as if she was talking to her husband. "But what if someone asks me who I am or why I am here. I guess I would wait outside your building. You come down after your shower and then we will go in together," I did not want to end up in news headlines for all the wrong reasons so I decided to take some precautions. "*Arre baba* no one is at home so no one is going to ask you anything. You just come up. I will take some twenty minutes," she said that and then she disconnected the phone.

I was in two minds. Whether it was a bait or it was my lucky day. I was there at the right time for an interesting encounter. Things couldn't have been better. I would be there inside her room and she would come out after shower draped in her wet towel, with droplets of water dripping from her entire body. That feeling was enough to make me decide the right course of action. I decided to give myself a chance.

The door was indeed unlatched. I moved inside and slowly called her name, "Jhilmil." There was no reply. This was my lucky day. I closed the door behind me and passed through the hall into the bedroom. There was a crumpled bed sheet and a night suit lying on the bed. The sprinkling sound of water was coming from inside the shower. This was all very filmy. Just the thought of what would happen next was making me excited.

What followed was much more exciting and thrilling as compared to my measly expectations. The door bell rang. All my excitement vanished in a moment. I had no experience of being in such a situation before so I decided to ignore my wisdom and turn to Jhilmil for guidance. I knocked at the bathroom's door, "Jhilmil door bell is ringing. What should I do?" The sound of shower stopped. She was done with her bath, "just ignore it. Whoever it is will think no one is at home and leave." "I felt some respite. I was in the right house with the right person for the right job. I ignored the door bell and started waiting eagerly for her to come out in that wet bath towel.

I guess the individual at the door knew that someone was inside the house. The door bell kept ringing continuously. I had begun to feel nervous now. Jhilmil moved out of the bathroom. To my utter dismay she was not in her towel but dressed from head to toe in a jeans and T-shirt. She had a look of fear on her face. I had an inkling now that I was in midst of some big trouble. "Who is it?" I asked her. "No one. Just keep quiet. Don't make any sound. He will go by himself," she was visibly worried. I had nothing better to do than follow her advice. I had no expectations left. I just wanted to move out of that place as quickly as possible and run back to my campus.

Door bell stopped ringing. Instead that person started banging at the door. "Jhilmil I know you are inside with him.

Open the door." A very angry voice came from outside the house. "There is no one here. I am alone at home. You please leave,'" Jhilmil was telling that guy. "Don't lie to me. I know you have called him. His name is Satyam, right? I will kill him today." I do not know what effect this revelation had on Jhilmil but it certainly did not have a very good impact on me. I started shivering. I went to the kitchen and took out the biggest knife I could see. I did not want to die a bachelor and so I started preparing myself mentally for what seemed inevitable. "Who Satyam? There is no one here. Now please do not create a scene here. What will my neighbours think? It is because of this attitude of yours that I don't like talking to you. Now please leave or I will call the security guards," she tried to threaten him. "If no one is inside why are you not opening the door? Open the door once, I will just see inside and leave. I would not say anything to you." I guess he was being reasonable but his reasoning was going to put me in big trouble. I already was in big trouble. "No you are very angry right now. You will hurt me. I would not open the door. You go and give your exam," this girl had guts. She was still holding on to her stance even when it was evident that the guy knew I was inside. "No I would not give my exam. I will keep waiting here till your mom returns. You will have to open the gate then. We will know then who is right and who is wrong," that guy was determined to settle the matter.

I had lost all hope of getting out of the situation. There was nothing I could do. That was time for me to pay for the sin that I had not even committed. If that guy had to turn up could not he have waited for an hour or so? I would have been much happier facing the consequences then. What can a small entity like I do when all the forces of nature decide to have some fun on its expense? There was only one thing to do, wait and watch. I was doing exactly that. "Listen, don't drag our parents into this. You dare not do anything like that," this was Jhilmil's turn to shout. "Then open the door for five minutes," he was ordering now. "No I would not. You leave." "If you would not, then I will break the door," he said that and then started giving heavy blows to the door. This was turning ugly now and if nothing was done fast one of us was sure going to end up into dead meat. "Call the security," I told Jhilmil. She called the security and told them that someone was trying to enter her house. Security guards came. By the noises outside we could make out that he was being dragged away. He shouted as he left, "Satyam you will die soon."

The moment the drama was over I turned to Jhilmil, "what the fuck is going on here?" "I am sorry. Please don't feel bad. I did not know he will come here. He had an exam today." "But who is he?" I had many questions that needed answers. "He is my ex-boy-friend," she told me. "If he is your ex-boyfriend then how does it matter to him that with who you are and what you are doing," I had completely forgotten my original purpose of being there. What now really mattered was to know how real that guy's threats were. "I mean we have not broken up yet but we are on the verge of breaking up," she corrected herself. "What do you mean? You already have a boyfriend and you called me home alone and you did not even tell me about that. Are you nuts?" I had valid reasons to be angry at her. I was being dragged into a quagmire and she did not even bother to take my consent for the same. "I am sorry. I thought I will meet you first and when things click between us then I will break-up with my boyfriend," she said that so innocently that even I wondered for a while if she actually meant that. I decided it would be better to confirm, "You mean to say if you would become my girlfriend then you will ditch him else you will continue with him. Is this what you mean?" "No, I meant that there was no point bothering you telling about my issues unless I was sure that our relation was going to be a longer one. I did not know he would come here. I am sorry." "See I have no interest in coming between you two lovers. First you settle your affairs with him, whatever it is and only then you contact me," I told her plainly. Though I was looking for some fun but I did not want to achieve that at the expense of someone's relation. I had thought she was single and I was mistaken. "Ok," she said that in such a sad tone as if my statement was a big blow to her. "Now tell me how that guy knew that I would be coming here at this time and how did he know my name?" these were the most pertinent questions whose answers I needed badly. "I have no clue. Even I am wondering," she told me with a plain face. "Ok. Do you think he would be outside now? I would want to leave now," I told her. "No he has an exam in fifteen minutes. You can leave safely. But why are you leaving now. Stay for some more time please," she pleaded. "No, I just want to move out of this shit fast," I told her as I began to leave.

Before I could step out of her bedroom my phone rang. It was an unknown number. I answered the call. Someone was in a very bad mood, "*Aaj to tujhe Jhilmil ne bacha liya bacche par ab tu ulti ginti ginnna chalu kar de. Dus din. Sirf dus din ki jindagi aur hai teri.* The moment my exams get over I will kill you." I turned the speaker phone on so that Jhilmil also knows what type of soup she had put me in. "Listen, I had no," I tried to explain to him but he did not let me complete. "No, not me, but you listen now. *Jahan bhagna hai bhag ja. Tujhe kahin se bhi nikal ke maroonga main,*" he had not taken well to his girlfriend being with me in her own house and that too alone. "*Pehle tu ye decide kar ki tere ko baat karne ka hai ki maarne ka hai. Agar maarne ka hai to mai phone rakh raha hoon. Mere paas fokat ka time nahi hai.* If you want to talk then tell me," I gave him back in his own coin. It worked. He was ready to talk now. "Speak," he said. "Yes I was at Jhilmil's house but I did not know she had a boyfriend. We are just good friends. There is nothing between us and we did not do anything," I told him the truth. "I am not a fool to trust you. If you people had nothing to hide why did not you open the door? These excuses will not spare you from me." "See Mr. if I had to make an excuse I would never have told you that I was at her house. As for not opening the door I have already told you that I did not know she had a boyfriend. I had no clue of what was happening and so there was no reason for me to come between you two," I tried to explain things to him but he was not in a state to understand anything. "*Beta beech mai to tu aa hi gaya hai hum dono ke.* She has been my girlfriend for last ten years. Think about it, if she is ready to leave me just because she met an IIM guy; what she will do to you when she finds someone better. I am telling you for your own good. Leave her," he was advising me now on why his girlfriend could not be an ideal girlfriend for me! "I am trying to make you understand the same thing my friend. She is not my girlfriend and I do not love her. It was for the first time I met her and had I known she already had a boyfriend I would not even have met her. Now since I know you are her boyfriend I have told her that we will not meet until you people sort out your affairs," he was giving me an ear now. He had definitely cooled down a bit. I tried to make him more comfortable, "Friend, even my girl friend had ditched me. So I know the pain you are undergoing. Had I known about you I would never have met her in the first place." I guess he was beginning to trust me now. "Are you still at her place," he asked. "No, I have already left. I am in my campus," I lied but then it was irrelevant to him. "Ok. I hope you keep your word," he told me in a threatening tone. "Of course I will." I disconnected.

I turned to Jhilmil, "Ma'am, not even my name, he knows my phone number as well. Don't tell me you don't know how he got it." "I swear I have no clue," she touched her throat. "But we have only chatted once, how can he know all the details? Is he spying on you?" "Why would he spy on me? He already knows all my passwords," she told it so proudly that if I had it in my powers I would have awarded her Nobel prize for honesty. "If he has your password he can read your chats. Is it too difficult to guess?" I was shocked at her stupidity. "Oh, yes. How can I forget that? This is how he got your number. Right?" she wondered. I did not know whether to laugh or cry at her question. "Are you sure? No, that cannot be true. If he has your password how he can read your chat with that," I meant each single word of the sarcasm. "Yes you are right. How can he read my chats? He only has my mail password? I guess he is actually spying on me," she was actually serious when she said that. There was nothing I could say or add. I bid her good bye and told her not to contact me until she sorted out with her boyfriend first.

I was happy I walked out of that situation unhurt and alive. I decided at that very moment that no matter what, I was not going to try such adventures again. I already had a girlfriend, so what if she was miles apart. Moreover my life was too precious for these cheap thrills.

THE BEGINNING OF THE END

36

Though I did try to develop feelings for Zora but I was failing in that. We had spent a lot of time together, shared many a moment; both happy and sad, still I felt there was something lacking in our relation. At times I felt like even after being so close we were complete strangers to each other. She never completely opened up with me and even I could not open up with her the way I could with Anisha. With Anisha that happened by itself. I never really had to make any efforts for that but with Zora even after trying from my side I could not share my feelings. I knew she loved me, I knew she cared a lot for me but despite trying I could never feel the same towards her. I guess relations do not work this way. You can not really mould them by design. They should better be left free and you should watch just watch them grow and embrace them. I believe this is the only key to successful relations.

Ever since Anisha had come back in my life I was undergoing a change. Though I always had a soft corner for her but now I was not in love with her. There was a long period when we had not talked and though I did miss her at times but I had moved out of her. Still things were happening that were shaking my faith in myself. I could not find time to talk to Zora but I would be willing to talk to Anisha even a day before my exam. Though she had always been more important than Zora but was it only friendship or did I still feel for her? I had started having doubts about that however I never shared any of my dilemmas with her. She already had enough troubles of her own and my only concern was to help her out of them, even at the expense of creating distance between us.

I did not really know why I was helping Anisha in getting away from me. Every other day she would discuss with me some problem that she was facing in her relation and I would try to help her out of that. Every time I helped things smoothen between Anisha and Martin I was sending her away from me. It was not that I did not know the implications but still I was doing that. Even if I felt Martin was wrong in something I will never tell that to Anisha, rather I would suggest her to talk to him and understand his view point.

One reason why I was helping Anisha, could be that her expectations with me were so high that I could never let her down. For her I was her best-friend, no not even best-friend but much more than that. 'If there ever will be a relationship in my life that I will value more than anything else, it will be our relation. Even the relationship of husband-wife can not be as pristine as our relationship is' she had told me once. I was always confused by this or I guess she was confused, she did not understand what she wanted. If this relationship was so important to her then why had she turned me down? I never got to know the answer to this because I never posed this question to her. How could I? That was a difficult question. That would pain her a lot and I could not give her any pain. Not even in my dreams. They say that everything is fair in love and war but the way she counted on me, the way she left herself to my whims when she discussed her problems with me there was no way I could tell her anything else but what will reduce her pain. May be that is why I always helped her in all her issues.

Another reason could be that she had changed during all this time. She was no longer the Anisha whom I had always looked up to. Rather she had become weak. Though she did discuss her problems with me earlier as well but that used to happen only once in a while and even when she did discuss, the intent was not to seek guidance but just to have someone to share her feelings with. This is the frailty of human emotions. Even when you know that the other individual would not do anything more than listen to you patiently, still you find comfort in the realization that there is someone who understands your reasons and the problems fail to bother you anymore. May be one reason why I was still helping her was that I realized that she had grown weak and she genuinely needed help. She was vulnerable and how could I leave her to herself in such a situation.

One more reason could be that I had faith in my feelings. I had trust in my love. I always knew she loved me as well but it was for her to realize that she did and I was willing to wait until she realized that. I never felt insecure about that so there was no question of mine not helping her. May be by going close to Martin she will actually realize what she is leaving behind. May be then she will realize if she actually wants to spend her life with me and in the end if she did realize that I was wrong, if she did realize that she wishes to spend her life with Martin and not me, even then I would have helped her in finding her right match. My stand would still be vindicated.

To be completely honest to myself I did not know what exactly the reason was. Any of the above three or all the three or anything else but one thing about which I was sure was that either I was again falling for her or I had never fallen out of her love in the first place.

37

Unlike my mid term exams, the end term exams did not go well. I was losing focus in studies. Till it was necessary to attend the tutorials I used to study but once it became optional I started spending most of the time in watching movies and playing games. It was not that I did not try to study at all. I did, but things were very difficult, especially Statistics. After banging my head on it for 3-4 hours I was never left with any energy to study anything else. Somehow I wrote the exams. Finally the first term in IIM C was over.

After my last exam when I reached back to the hostel an entirely new event was awaiting us. They called it 'The World War.' It was a 60 hour long non stop Intra Hostel competition involving a plethora of activities ranging from fancy dress, drama, balloon throwing and athletics to name a few. In all some thirty activities were conducted back to back. There were no inhibitions. All the silly things that we ever dreamt of doing in our childhood; we could do them now. Though it was extremely tiring but it was too irresistible to stay away from. By the end of the event I did not have energy even to lift a finger.

The games lasted till 3 A.M. on Monday. After spending three sleepless nights I desperately wanted to rest. No sooner had I hit the bed that I went to sleep. With great difficulty I woke up in the morning. I was planning to miss the lecture and sleep but Rick had told that first term results were up on the notice board so I changed my mind. By the time I reached the academic block I was running late for the class. I decided to attend the lecture first and then check my result. I reached a bit late but the professor allowed me inside. A Human Resource case was being discussed in the class. After three days of toil most of the students were resting in their beds. Almost half of the seats were vacant. Most amongst those who were present were sleepy and no one was really participating in the discussion. This went on for some time after which the faculty got irritated. He left the class without completing the topic and tore down the attendance sheet. It was not a good start. The students who were resting in their beds were much better than us. It was for the sake of attendance that we took all troubles to come to the class and finally we were denied that. This was not the first time it was happening. Faculty had made it a habit to use attendance as an instrument to discipline the students. It did not feel right.

I moved out of the lecture hall and went to check my results. A large crowd had gathered around the notice board to know their results. There were rumours that some fifteen students had flunked in Statistics. Rumours were wrong. Actually nineteen students had flunked in Statistics. I was one of them. I had scored above average grades in rest of the subjects but it did not matter. I was a failure. Though I had never taken studies very seriously but it was the first time I had flunked in a subject. Somehow I had always managed to sail through till now but MBA was a different ball game. The result was there on the notice board for every one to see. All new friends I had made during last three days will now know that I was a failure. No intelligent student would ever talk to me. I will be treated as an outcaste. I had been through many embarrassing situations before but none of them were any match to the feeling of being treated as a failure by everyone. I did not have the courage to face all this. I went straight back to my hostel room and switched off the lights. I wanted to be left alone. I tried sleeping but I could not. I had not slept properly since the end term exams had started. I had a severe headache. I missed my lunch and dinner. I kept lying in my bed for what seemed like eternity. It was long past midnight when I finally slept.

38

I was woken up by the noise of heavy banging at my door. It was one 'O Clock. I had slept through noon and missed all the morning sessions. Rick was calling my name and banging heavily on the door. "What is the matter with you man," I asked him as I opened the door. Rick looked exhausted. He was gasping heavily. It seemed like he had come straight after running a marathon. "What is the matter with me?" he literally shouted at me, "What is the matter with you man? Why did not you come to class? Where have you been since yesterday?" I did not understand why he was over reacting. It was not such a big deal. I told him to come inside and offered him some water. "What happened? Tell me calmly," I told him. He sat down and gulped down the water in one sip. "I was worried for you," he told me. "For me. But why?"

"I thought you had done something to yourself," he was still panting. His thoughts seemed insane to me. "You mean I would have committed suicide. You are insane man. Mark my word. I am not going to die a bachelor," I started laughing but Rick did not take it very well, "It is not a joke Satyam. You have been nowhere since yesterday. If you are not feeling good you should talk to someone. This is not the way that you lock yourself up in your room and cut off from everyone else." Till now I was trying to avoid the topic but now Rick had touched it and that too in a very blunt manner. I did not appreciate that at all. "What should have I talked to someone? Whom should have I talked to? I am a failure, ok. Understand that I am a failure. I have accepted that and no matter what you say, words do not help. It is a fact that I am a failure," I shouted back. Rick kept looking at me. He had not expected that reaction from me. "It is time for HR class. Come. You have already missed three lectures. Now don't miss any more attendances," he advised me. "How does it matter? I am anyway a failure. Why should I attend those classes? It is just a waste of time," I told Rick. "Go to hell. I am not going to miss my attendance because of you," Rick lost his temper and barged out of the room. I can not really blame him for this. He was just a bit concerned for me but I wanted to be left alone. After he left I plugged in my laptop. I had not checked any mails since the World War had started.

There were many unread mails but the one that drew my immediate attention was from Zora - subject 'Good Bye'
Dear Satyam,
Hope you are having a blast as always.

I have thought a lot about this and I believe this is the time for us to bid adieu. I know this is what you want but you will never have the guts to say it out. So, here I am, making it easier for you. You don't need to feel guilty about it ever. It is not your decision but mine. The only regret I have is the way you showed me my place.

I understand you were busy for your exams but now it has been four days since your exams ended and I am tired of dialling your number again and again. I know you have changed your phone number but trust me there was no need for you to do that. If you had just told me once that you want me out of your life, I would have obliged happily. But all that does not matter now.

May you become a successful manager.

Yours Always

0.

    I was dead tired after 'The World War', had not slept for days and flunked in first term exams. This mail was the last thing that I needed. I switched on the cell phone and called Zora. The moment she answered the call I shouted at her, "What the hell does your mail mean?" "I am in my office Satyam. Can we talk later," Zora replied in a very low voice. "You know what. Go to hell." I disconnected the phone and continued surfing through my mails. There was one from Academic Representatives of Student Council. The mail was marked to some thirty odd students. We were told to assemble in Lecture hall at 10 PM 'to discuss some important issue.' I knew at least five people in the cc list. They too had flunked in Statistics. I started wondering what these people were up

to. Were they going to outcaste us? What was the point in calling all of us together? So that everyone knows that we are failures, a black spot on the face of this temple of learning. I definitely was not looking forward to this session but there was no choice. If I did not attend that I would be levied a fine. The Student Council had the right to impose fine upon anyone not following its diktats. Things were already too bad and now they were taking a turn for the worst. I desperately wanted to talk to someone. I wanted to talk to Anisha. She was the only one who could understand me, who could comfort me, who was not demanding at all. I logged on to the chat application but Anisha was not online. Jhilmil was online. I desperately wanted a distraction. I pinged her
Hi Jhilmil.
Hi.
How are things between you and your bf?
We are no longer together, we just talk sometimes.
Is he ok with that?
Yes, he is now. Anyway, leave him, what about you?
Nothing much, Just passing life.
You seem bored, you need some excitement man.
Yes I know that. But where do I get that?
Wherever you want, let's meet, what do you say?
I don't love you. Neither am I looking for a long term relationship with you.
I know that
Then
Then what?

I mean excitement... am not looking for any commitment, just a diversion.
Do you think I am looking for a commitment?
But you said so last time we met?
Forget all what I said last time. This is a new time, isn't it?
I don't know.
Ok. Let me know when you know. Bye.
You can't go like this. Talk to me
[Enigma99 is offline. Messages you send will be delivered when Enigma99 comes online]

This was turning out to be the worst day of my life. Every time I felt that I had already seen the worst, I was proven wrong. With each passing moment things kept on deteriorating. I did not know how much more was still in store for me. Time had slowed down. I did not want to step out of my room but I had nothing to do while sitting inside there. I was feeling hungry. I went down to the canteen and brought some chips and sandwiches. No one was there in the quad. People had not yet returned from the lectures. I again moved back to my room. I put on a French movie on my laptop, not because I understood French but precisely because I did not understand French. I did not want a single cell of my brain to waste any efforts in watching a flick that it could understand. By the time movie was complete it was dark outside. I was feeling suffocated in my closed room. I stepped out of my room and walked towards the howrah bridge. It would be desolated at this hour. A cool breeze was blowing across the lake. There was no human noise in the vicinity, just the pleasing sound of birds chirping in the evening. I had been in that campus for a little over three months now but never before did I stop to look at the beauty and calm that the campus offered. I had always been too busy to complete the next assignment, meet the next deadline, prepare the next presentation that I hardly got any time to relax and take note of what I was missing in this race for getting more marks. Even when I was not studying, I was in my room either watching movies or playing games while the nature outside had so much to offer. I sat quietly at the corner of the bridge, letting my legs hang loosely in the air. There was no highway, no headlights but a pitch dark silence and cool gusts of winds that came at irregular intervals. It was soothing in a unique way. After a long time was I feeling a little relaxed. I kept sitting there for around an hour. The silence was broken by the ringing of my cell phone.

"You don't have any right to shout at me. Though I am not as busy as you are but even I have my own life. You can not just call me in my office and shout at me." Zora was on the call and I could make out she was determined to fight. However I was not in a mood to fight now. I did not reply. She waited for a while and then continued, "Satyam, talk to me. Why have you done this?" "Done what?" I asked. She shouted over the phone, "you know what, you have used me." Though I did not want to get involved in any new altercation but I could not take that baseless allegation on me. "What do you mean by I have used you? It was you who mailed me saying you want to part ways. Don't put it on me now," I told her in very clear terms. "Listen Mr. It was you who did not take my calls since last four days. You were supposed to call me at least once after your exams were over. I had no way to know even if you were dead or alive. What would you expect me to do in such a situation?" "I will tell you what you should do in such a situation. In such a situation you should write a mail saying we are parting ways. Right? This is what you should do," I replied. Though I only told her that what she did was right but probably she had not expected that answer. Whatever it was, the answer did not go well with her and she shouted again, "Don't talk bullshit. Tell me why your phone was switched off." Till now I was trying to retain my calm but it was becoming increasingly difficult now. "Listen, when I switch my phone on or when I switch my phone off is none of your business. I don't spy on you what you are doing when and you also stop doing it. I need my space. Ok?" "How much more space do you need yaar? I don't call you; it has been months since we met and weeks since we talked. How much more space you need?" Her voice had mellowed down now. "A lot more space. I don't need these tensions, I don't need these fights and I don't need this answerability to you on why I call you or why I don't call you. You do whatever you want to do and I will do whatever I want to do," I replied. "Do you mean you want to break off?" her voice was very calm now. "What break off *yaar*. I am just saying I need some space. Anyway you are in Noida and I am in Calcutta. Just let this phase pass by. Things will themselves get normal," I told her. She kept quiet for a long time. Then she spoke, "Satyam, I guess you need to decide now whether you want me in your life or not." "Of course I want you in my life *yaar*," I replied. "No, not that ways. What

I mean is whether you want to marry me or not." That was a tough question for me. Though I did like her but my feelings never developed to the extent of conviction for marriage. "I have not been able to decide till now. I will need more time," I told her frankly. But Zora was not ready to be in a dicey state any more. "You already had a lot of time. I guess you should have decided by now. You can tell me your decision whatever it is," she told me. "No, frankly speaking I have not been able to decide till now in either direction. But if you want me to make a decision now I will say No," I replied. A long silence followed. After some time she spoke. Her voice heavy, "if I give you more time is there a possibility that you will decide in my favour." "Yes there is. But there is also a possibility of me not deciding in your favour," I told her. "I know that. How much time do you need?" she had started sobbing now. "I don't really know. But whatever it is I will give you my answer in a month's time." "Ok. I will call you after a month then." She disconnected the phone.

The watch was showing a quarter pass nine. I had to go for that academic representative's session at ten. I started walking back towards the hostel. I had to shave and take a shower before I would go for that session. I don't know the exact reason for the same but I was feeling a bit light now.

39

A total of thirty five students had assembled in the lecture hall including three student council representatives for academic affairs. If my guess was correct then this meant that thirty two of us had flunked in one or more subjects. There were some known and many unknown faces in the gathering but quite unlike a normal crowd at IIM none of them was talking. All of them were quietly sitting at their places trying not to look at or talk to anyone else. All of those warriors who just a few days ago were epitome of confidence suddenly looked like defeated minnows. Perhaps all of us knew why we had been called there but none of us wanted to face the stigma of being identified as a failure.

"Do you know why all of you are here?" Vishal spoke. He was the youngest one of the three member academic council team. No one replied. "Do you know three students have been asked to withdraw permanently from the course?" he further asked. Murmurs started among students. "How many of you have read the rule book?" It seemed like Vishal had come prepared with a set of questionnaire for us but none of us were offering him any replies. I had no clue of what he was getting at but the confusion did not last long. "Three students have been asked to withdraw from the program because they flunked in three subjects," he finally told us. "At any point of time during the course if you flunk in more than two subjects you are automatically out of the institution. Three students are already out and among you all twelve have already flunked in two subjects and twenty in one. Just one or two more failures and you will be out of this institute forever."

There was a pin drop silence. I did not know of this rule before and I am sure many others were also in the same boat as me. Vishal started speaking again, "Please understand we are not here to scare you but we are here to help you. We have decided to start special tutorial sessions for you. We have taken a feedback from your tutors and figured out that many of you are unable to take much from the regular tutorial sessions because of large batch sizes and also because you do not ask many questions in these sessions and so we have decided that these special tutorial sessions for you will be conducted by students from your own batch and only you people will be allowed to attend these sessions so that class size is limited and you can draw maximum benefit out of it. Also it is not mandatory for you to attend the sessions but in case you choose not to attend these we might not be able to help you in any way later on."

I found that ridiculous. I was an adult and I wanted to be treated like an adult. Whether I wanted to study or not, that was my calling. Who gave him the right to impose his whims on me and also on everyone else? We were already broken by the results and now these people were making us realize that our days in the institute were limited. Now we will be known as special people who have special tutorials. Everyone will know that we are failures, even those who had not read our names at the notice board will now know that we are failures. To add to the injury our friends with whom we sit next to next in the lectures, they will be conducting these sessions. Even they will start treating us as failures now. How easily had he said we are trying to help you people and what did he mean by you people? Was he much above us? We both got admitted into the same institute, we both wrote the same exam, we both went through the same interview process and now we are here listening to him quietly when he is labelling us as you people. Why does he not use the term you failures instead?

After Vishal was done he opened the floor for questions and all three of them started replying to individual queries. I got to know a lot of new things through that process. I got to know that there was no scope for re-test in any subject. A failure once means a failure forever. Also there was no concept of absolute passing marks, it was all relative marks. So even if you score fifty percent in a course you could still flunk if everyone else scores more than you. Also there was no concept of rounding up. Whether you stay in the institute or not could be decided by a factor of as minute as 0.25 marks. Now I realized why everyone was always vying for that extra mark. Even I should have done that.

That covered almost everything that was discussed in the session but still one question merits a special mention. That gentleman had read that question from his notebook. Either he had written it himself because he wanted to be sure of not missing a single word or probably someone had written that question and given it to him to ask in that forum. "Almost ninety five percent of people who have flunked are from reserved categories, all three who have been asked to withdraw are also from reserved category. Till last year hardly one or two students flunked in any course but this year nineteen students flunked in Statistics. Till last year hardly one or two students were made to drop out of the program for flunking in more than two subjects but this year three students have already dropped out and if the trend continues many more will follow. Why is there such a huge increase in number of failures this year? Is it because of the reservations imposed by Government? Is it the IIMs way of telling the Government that who is the boss?" It was unbelievable. That person must have had guts of iron to ask that question openly in that forum. Students started thumping the desk as soon as the question was over. The three academic representatives started discussing something in close loop. Obviously they were not prepared for such a blatant question.

Finally Vishal came ahead once again, "About the increase in number of failures vis-à-vis previous years, I have to admit that we don't have any data on that. Though I am not saying that it could not have happened but whatever it is I can assure you it has got nothing to do with any thing other than your academic performance. Please understand that in the same batch there are students who have scored 99.99 percentile and there are those who scored 80 percentile. Once into the institute all of them compete on same parameters from day one and it is true that some will get more marks and some will get less. You can not expect the gap of 20 percentile points to bridge in one day but the least we can do is to try to bridge this gap. In a relative grading system like the one we follow it is bound to happen that the performance of a 99 percentiler will affect the performance of a 80 percentiler. In such a case rather than trying to attribute our success or blame our failures to external causes it is best that we try to reach the performance level of a 99 percentiler and bridge the gap to such a small number that none of us flunks. Gentleman, whatever you have said might make a good plot for conspiracy theory. When I speak I vouch not only for all three of us but for the entire student council. Let me assure you that whether you pass or fail is not determined by anything else but your academic performance otherwise not even a single non reservation student would ever flunk. So the best thing to do is not to listen to these theories but to work hard and improve our performance. IIM C of all management institutes follows the most transparent performance evaluation system. All of you get to see your copies and you can even compare your answer sheets with those of other students. As such there is no scope of anyone getting different marks for same answer. Please remove all biased notions from your mind, don't listen to any rumours and just focus on your performance. If you need any help, call any of us at any hour of day or night and let me assure you if you give your best no one can stop you from passing with flying colours and getting the best this campus has to offer." His speech was greeted with loud thumps, much louder than those generated by the question. The thumps lasted non stop for almost two minutes after which the session was declared over.

Though initially I had felt that this session was a way to humiliate us but now I knew it was not that. Listening to Vishal I could feel his concern for everyone present there. He was right, I was not from any reserved background still I had flunked and I could not blame it to anything else but my lack of preparation. Had I studied more seriously at my graduation level I would not have flunked in Statistics. There was no Avash to help me with that here. But still these special tutorial sessions might help. In my thoughts I thanked the gentleman who had raised that question for it was only because of that question being asked that I now gained a little confidence in the intentions and attitude of the academic representatives.

40

As I moved out of the lecture hall and started walking towards the hostel, I decided to call Avash. It had been almost a month since we had talked last. He definitely would not know about Anisha. Also I had to give him the news of my greatest achievement, flunking in IIM. "Hey Avash, how was your summers internship? Any news on the Pre Placement Offer?" Avash had done his summer internship with J P Morgan, London in their investment banking division. "Summers was good yaar, I am expecting a PPO. Let us see," he told me. "That is good news man. Hope you get the PPO. What about the enjoyment part? What did you do in Europe? Did you go to Amsterdam? Have heard it is the sex capital of Europe!" Avash started chuckling, "General Knowledge *kafee badh gayi hai aapki dost*. No I did not go to Amsterdam. I toured Scotland, Germany, France, Switzerland and Italy. There was not much time to roam *yaar*." "Oh yes! Not much time to roam so you had to content yourself with little places like Switzerland, France, Germany, Italy etc., right?" I commented. "Bang on my dear friend," he started laughing, "tell me what is going on in your life? Your first term must be over by now? When are your summer's interviews starting?" "Well, things are not very rosy here. Got a *fucca* in Statistics," I replied. His tone changed as he heard that news, "And what about your summer internship? When is the process starting and how is your preparation for that?" "No *yaar* I have not prepared anything, neither am I planning to do so and about the process I guess it would start in a month's time," I told him. "Don't be stupid Satyam, you never know what you can get. It is just a question of one interview. So do prepare for it," he started advising me but I had called him not to discuss all this but something of more importance. "Leave this topic Avash. I want to tell you something." "Yes, tell me," Avash replied. "I met Anisha online," I told him and kept quiet to give him sufficient time to digest the information. "Ok," he replied. I waited for him to continue the conversation but he did not utter a single word further. "She is getting married," I told him. This time the reply was instantaneous, "when and to whom?" "The date is not fixed yet and as far as with whom is concerned I don't know much about him but he is some family friend. I thought I would let you know. I guess you should move on now." "Thanks for telling," he replied in a bland tone. I was not able to get any reaction from him. It seemed as the news did not matter to him at all. "Shall I give you her chat id? Would you like to talk to her?" I asked him.

"No, I don't want to talk to her," he replied. The news surely did matter to him. He was still in love with her. I could not think of anything else to talk about and I knew talking about her will make him feel worse. Even he was quiet. Both of us were waiting for each other to continue the conversation but we did not know what to talk about at that moment. Finally we disconnected the call.

I had a choice to make, whether to focus on my studies or prepare for summers. The latter was a question of my self respect and confidence while the former was a question of my very survival in the institute. If only I could manage a good summers and convert it into placement offer then whatever grades I get at college would not matter as long as I clear the course. However if I fail to pass the program then summers would not matter. If I could not manage to get a PPO and pass with bad grades at college my future would be doomed in that case as well. However none of these criteria helped me in making the right choice though. What actually helped was the fact that for summers I would have to toil for only one month while for getting good grades the effort required would be exponential and that too over an extended period of time. Mid term exams were scheduled a week after the summer placement process. A week would be sufficient to brace through in courses apart from Statistics – part II; the devil that was still after my life, however the devil would be taken care of during the end terms. I decided mentally and started preparing for the summers. That was the only thing I was going to do for next one month.

THE CROSSROAD

41

In retrospect, I can claim without any doubts that no matter what field you major in, the biggest take away from any management program is the Art of Resume Making. It was after some seven days and a score of revisions by dozens of seniors that I was finally satisfied with my resume. It was only after I read it completely that I realized how much potential I had. All of a sudden, things which always seemed so irrelevant, they appeared like the greatest achievements one could ever dream of. Frankly speaking, having known myself; if I had the authority, I would never have hired me but given what my resume spoke I would now be forced to do the opposite. Satisfied with my resume I mailed it to many of my friends asking for their suggestions. Actually it was not that I was looking for any suggestions, I just wanted them to know how much potential I had, I wanted to know if they would be as surprised looking at my resume as I was. A lot of them did get amused but Anisha did not. 'She always knew I had that much potential,' She had once told me.

So which firms are you aiming at?

Don't know yet, probably all of them but for I-banks.

Why not I-banks?

Would not get any calls from them so no point trying.

But why do you think that ways? You have such a good resume.

People have better and anyway that is not the type of life I want.

And what is it that you want?

I just want a 6-8 hrs. job and then enjoy rest of the time. What is the point in earning so much if I won't have time to spend it? Anyway sooner or later money would come; the important thing is that I should do what I like to do and not what pays more.

You are right. Once you get settled take a home near us. We will roam out on weekends together.

Your husband would allow that?

Why not? He knows you are my best friend and he understands your importance in my life.

☺

What happened? You don't trust me on this?

Leave it.

No tell me, please.

I am not only your best friend. I love you as well.

So what, even I love you but that is platonic love.

And you think he would understand that?
Yes.
☺

☹ My marriage date has been fixed.
Congrats
Won't you ask which date?
No.
Are you not going to attend my wedding?
No.
If you don't come I would not marry.
You would.
No, I would not.
Ok. Don't marry then.
Why are you doing this Satyam? How can you leave me alone at such a time? You know I need you.
I know that and that is why am leaving you alone. You should not need me anymore and by the way even I need you, much more than you need me but you are leaving me alone as well
Please don't say like this. You are making me cry. I am not leaving you. Once your studies are over we will stay close by, we will meet every week.
☺
You don't trust me. Do you?
I trust you but you don't trust yourself.
What do you mean?
You will know it yourself in some time, all the best for your marriage. I can not talk anymore. Do take care of yourself. Bye
All the best for your summers, you take care too. Bye

Sooner or later it had to happen but I never knew it would cause so much pain. In that one moment I understood myself a lot better. I was not strong. I only used to act as if I was. The feeling of being away from her forever; the realization that I will not be able to talk to her, to call her, to be with her at my will, it was breaking me down. After a long time I was crying. I was going to lose her, forever. I desperately wanted to talk to someone. I wanted a shoulder to cry on but there was no one with whom I could share my feelings. I could not tell all this to Avash, I was his best friend. I could not talk to Zora, she herself was in love with me. Talking to Anisha was out of question. I had to bear this alone.

42

Only one week was left before the summer placement process would begin. I-Banks had already started coming up with their shortlists. Rick had got seven shortlists so far. I had not applied to any of them. My count was zero. More than fifty percent of the students had got slot Zero shortlists –interviews on the first day of placement process. This is the day when all the top paying foreign firms come to the campus for placements. They get to check all the candidates and select the best of the breed. The leftovers then go through placement process of lesser ranked firms on day one or two or three as the case may be. Many a times people with slot zero calls could not convert their interviews and then go through subsequent slots with lesser mortals who did not have any slot zero calls. This could be very painful in the end. However I avoided all that pain as I did not have any slot zero calls.

First day of placement was over. One-third of the batch got placed on the D-Day. There were mixed emotions on the campus. Those who got through were on top of the world. Those who could not were lost, some of them were crying. It was not that getting a day zero offer was all it meant to be successful but somehow with all the good news floating around you the pressure increases so much that you are unable to give your best performance. Those who could not make it on day zero were going to compete with us for the remaining offers from tomorrow onwards. Pressures were high and all of us were studying.

It was around ten in the night. I was about to hit the bed. My first day in summer process would start tomorrow at 7 AM. I wanted to have a good night's sleep and wake up fresh for the process but things do not always go as per your plan; with me they never do. Zora called up. More than a month had passed since she had given me that deadline but I had not answered her yet. I was never so sure about my feelings towards Zora. Sometimes I did feel that there might be a scope of developing feelings for her but after talking to Anisha that day, I knew that there was none. I could never really love Zora. Rather I could never really love anyone else but Anisha. I knew it would be harsh on Zora but the time had come for her to face it. There was no point in continuing giving her hope when I was now sure that it was not going to work out. "You did not call. It has been more than a month now," she spoke softly. "I am sorry for that. I was keeping quite busy." I did not know how to tell her what I was thinking. It required a lot of courage which I did not have. "Yes, I can understand.

Anyway, tell me have you decided?" she asked it straight without mincing any words. She was looking for a straight reply and though I had one I did not know how to deliver it so as to cause minimum damage to our relationship. "Well I have still not been able to convince myself about you and so I suggest you should not waste any more of your time. You should carry on," I tried to put it as harmlessly as was possible for me. She stayed quiet. That reaction was expected. I did not disturb her. After some time she took a deep breath and asked, "do you need more time to decide?" She did not want me to go away from her but then the longer I would stay the more painful it would be for her. There was no point in just delaying things. She had to face it one day and the sooner the better. "No, I feel you should move on now," I was determined to close the matter that day. "That means you are convinced that you do not want to stay with me. It is just that you can not accept it," she interpreted my answer for me. "No it is not like that, I have already told you that I am still not convinced whether I want to stay with you or not," I stuck to my stand. I wanted to avoid it but the discussion was slowly turning into an argument. "Then you can take your time until you decide," she wanted me to speak it out that I was ditching her but I was not ditching her at all. We never had a commitment and I wanted her not to bind herself to me. "I don't need any more time. I don't really think that I will ever feel for you from the marriage point of view. If it had to happen, it would have happened by now. No point just prolonging things and causing pain to each other. That is why I say you should move on." Zora kept thinking for a while.

She had still retained her calm. It was amazing. She never had that much patience. Probably she had already accepted our parting as a fact and so it was not affecting her. After a couple of minutes of silence she spoke, "Are you going around with someone?" I was afraid of this very thing. She must not feel that I was leaving her because of someone else. I could never feel for her long term. Though I always liked her but it never crossed the threshold of love. I never felt like spending my whole life with her and she knew that. "No," I replied. "Do you love someone else?" still calm, she asked the next question. "Is it necessary to discuss this?" I wanted to avoid this discussion at all cost. "Yes, it is important for me to know because of whom you are leaving me." "Zora don't take it that way *yaar*, I am not leaving you because of anyone else. It is just I could not ever feel like spending my entire life with you. What I feel for someone else has nothing to do with you," I was trying to reason out with her but at such a time when you know your loved one is being taken away from you, it is not the reasons but emotions that have the final say. "Tell me her name Satyam, I can take it" she replied. Finally I had to give up, "Anisha." She did not show any reaction, no surprise, no anger, nothing. "Since how long have you people been going around?" she asked me. I had already told her that I was not having an affair with anyone but probably she had forgotten that. I corrected her, "we are not going around. It is just that I feel for her. She does not feel for me. It is one sided, just like your and mine case." I added that to make her feel calm. If she was in pain so was I but it did not have the desired impact. "Since how long do you love her," her voice was breaking now. "Since college time," I replied. "But you had told me that Avash loved her," her voice had given way to tears now. It was going into a mess but I was unable to control it. "Yes he also loves her," I replied. "Does he know about you two?" she asked. "What is there to know about us two? I have already told you it is one sided feelings from my side only and what is the point in telling him when I know nothing is going to materialize. Why to pain him unnecessarily?" I was giving justifications while she had only asked a simple question, not any justifications. This was the first time I was talking about this subject and I guess the justifications were meant for me and not for anyone else. Zora was crying now. "You have used me Satyam. Why did you do this to me?" "I have not used anyone. How can you speak like this? You always knew I did not love you. Still I tried to think of you because I liked you. Don't try to make me feel guilty," I told her in clear terms. "Satyam you had feelings for her even before you met me but you never told me about that. You even slept with me while you still loved her and all this time I was under the impression that you love me. You have used me Satyam. I am feeling like a prostitute," she was crying regularly. At such a time it was difficult to reason out with her for she would not understand but still I tried, "Zora, listen to me calmly. Yes I did love her from college days but it was always one sided feeling and so there was no point in talking about something which did not have any chance to exist and as far as being with you is concerned we both liked being with each other. Whatever time we have spent together we did it because we both wanted to do that. I never forced you for anything and neither did you force me ever. Have you forgotten that we had decided that there would be no commitments? I have never told you that I love you. You always knew that so now you should not blame that on me. As far as being with you is concerned, you were and you are still my only girl friend. Though I agree I do love Anisha but she is not my girl friend, she never was and she never will be. Anyway she is getting married to somebody else very soon, if it gives you any comfort let me tell you that I am not doing it because I am going to marry her, I am doing it because I care for you and I feel there is no future for us together. So let us stay as friends and not spoil our friendship thinking about marriage." Zora was going through a lot of pain. She heard only what she wanted to hear. "So you are punishing me because she is marrying someone else. Since you could not get your love you will not let me get my love either. You know what, she is a bitch. She played with your heart all these years and now she is going to marry someone else and you are following suit. What she did to you, you are doing to me." There was no point discussing all this with her anymore. She was needlessly connecting things that had no relation at all. I raised my voice, "Mind your language Zora. If you don't want to understand then forget it. I have been trying to tell you everything and show the correct picture but you already have your pre conceived notions in your mind. You don't want to listen to anything. Whatever you think is right is right. When whatever I am telling you does not hold any value then why are you wasting my time. Do whatever you want to do, believe whatever you want to believe in but understand one thing, No matter what, I am not going to marry you." "Don't talk like this please. Don't shout at me Satyam. I love you. I can not live without you. I will die without you. Please give me a chance. Please," She was not ready to hear anything. This was not the right time to talk as I had my summers next day. "Do whatever you want to do. I don't want to talk to you," I shouted at her and then disconnected the phone. She called me again but I did not answer her call. I was already feeling bad because of losing Anisha. I switched off the cell phone and moved towards the howrah bridge. I needed to lighten up my mind before I could sleep.

43

Though I had five interviews on the first day I could not clear any. Next day I converted a decent offer. I got a role from Mittal steels in one of their Scandinavian projects. If nothing else, I would be able to see Europe. Rick had already landed up with Royal Bank of Scotland on day zero. So now both of us would be in Europe during our summers. The entire batch got placed on day two and so there was no reason why we would not celebrate. A party was organized to enjoy the successful completion of summer placement process. We drank and danced the whole night. Next day was a holiday so we could sleep whole day. We partied till morning and then we moved to our rooms. I switched on my cell phone and started checking my mails before hitting the bed. There was one mail from Zora but it was a very long one. It seemed like she had written for hours and hours at length. I had no energy to read such a long mail at that point of time. I hit the bed and slept instantly.

I had slept for a long time. By the time I woke up it was already dark outside. My laptop screen was open and Zora's mail was there. Though I knew what all it would contain and I had no intentions of getting together with her again but still I started going through it.

'Dear Satyam,

Forgive me for what I am doing but trust me had you been in my shoes you would have done the same.

No, I am not writing to beg you to be with me. I know you have already made up your mind so that is not possible now. I am writing because I just want to talk to you one final time. I am writing because you have barred my calls, you do not want to talk but still there are things that you must know. Even though, that would not matter after tomorrow.

Satyam, you never understood how much important you are to me. With you I have lost my only friend, my only relation, my only reason for living. Without you, I have nothing to live for but you would not understand that. Through this mail I am just trying to tell you about myself, a lot of things that you never knew. If after reading all this you feel that there is a scope for us to stay together then do get back to me else forget me altogether, forget that there ever was someone named Zora in your life. I will wait for your reply till 3 PM tomorrow. I don't have any reason to live apart from you. Please do forgive me but I can not tolerate this much pain. If I do not get your response by 3 PM tomorrow I will take sleeping pills.'

Zora had obviously gone mad. I did not know she would take such an extreme step just because of me. I checked the date the mail was written. She had written it yesterday. I looked at the watch. It was seven PM. There was nothing much I could do. I never had any faith in God but for the first time in my life I found myself praying to Him that everything should be fine. I dialled her number but no one answered. I could not think of what to do. My mind had stopped working. I called Anisha. "Anisha listen to me, take out your car and go to Zora's house, immediately." "What happened? Are you crying?" she replied. "Don't waste any time please, Zora has consumed sleeping pills. Please go there fast and get her some medical help," I pleaded to her. "Oh, but her house is far away. One of my uncle stays in that area. Give me the address. I will tell him to reach there and take her to a hospital; meanwhile I will also reach there. Don't worry, everything will be fine." I started crying. The feeling was making me sick. "*Khud ko sambhalo* Satyam. Everything is going to be fine. Have faith in God. I will give you a call once I reach there. Please take care of your self," Anisha said as she left for Zora's place. I was feeling handicapped sitting at that place. There was nothing I could do but cry. I was guilty towards Zora. Had I known it would result in this I would never have made friends with her. I had pushed her to the extreme and I could not even apologize to her now. There was nothing I could do but to pity myself and wait for Anisha's call. I continued reading her mail further.

'You never asked me much about my family and my past. I know you did not do it because you thought it will hurt me and you were right. It would definitely hurt me thinking of all that I have left behind but I would still like to share it with you today. There is no one else with whom I can share all this but you.

I told you that my parents died in an accident. That was not an accident. They were murdered. I had the best parents in this world but they were taken away from me, not by Allah but by man, by my own love. Yes, don't get shocked. I do have a past, a past that I would give anything to forget but that keeps on haunting me back and back. We were in same class. He was a Gujarati. His name was Hiren. We were madly in love with each other. We wanted to get married. We told this to our families but they were against inter religious marriage. Though I did love Hiren but not more than my parents so I told him that we could not marry and then one day he did that.

He took away my parents from me and then he killed himself. I had been a fool always. I loved the one who killed my parents. They died because of me. They always took care of me like a princess but I could never do anything for them. When they had opposed my marriage with Hiren I had fought with them, like mad and today when I want to apologize to them; they are no more. I have killed my parents and I deserve to die too but I could not do that. That would have been a very easy escape. I had to suffer. I had to punish my self much more severely until I can repent the sins I have committed and so I continued to live with that baggage on my shoulders.

I had stopped trusting people. When I could not trust

myself how could I trust anyone else? Then you came in my life. You were the only one who did not talk to me for my body, who was genuinely interested in me, who was honest, outright and a true friend. I still remember the moments that we had spent together, the letter that you wrote me then, the way you cared for me when I was sick. After a long time I could find someone in whom I could trust. Before meeting you I had forgotten what it means to trust someone, what it means to take care of someone and what it means to love someone. It was you who made me understand the meaning of all these things again. It was you who made me feel lively again. It was you who gave me a reason to live again. It was you who taught me to trust myself again but now you have gone. When you are not with me anymore what do I do? Whom do I trust in? Whom do I live for?

What you have done is right. I am a bad girl. I can only give pain. I have no right to live. And I know you never told me that you loved me but it was my fault, my stupidity that I loved you so much. This is not your fault at all but this had to happen. I deserve this pain. I deserve this punishment but I am happy that now it will end. I am going to meet my parents again.

Trust me I have no hard feelings for you. You taught me the meaning of life. You are the best human being I have ever met. I love you and I will always keep on loving you.

Forgive me for all the harsh words I have spoken.

Forgive me for all the pain I have given you.

Only Yours Forever

Zero.

I could not stop my tears. I never ever tried to understand her. Whatever was happening to her I was responsible for it and I could not do anything to stop that.

Anisha called me, "we have shifted her to Holy Family hospital. Doctor says there are fifty-fifty chances." "Thank you Anisha. I will catch the first flight and come there. Please do me a favour. Can you please stay there until I come?" I took my wallet and credit card and ran towards the taxi stand. "Of course dear, I am not going anywhere. Come safely. I will meet you at the hospital."

44

I reached the hospital at 1 A.M. Anisha was waiting for me in the lobby. "How is she now?" I asked her. "Still in the ICU, Doctors have told that if she does not come back to senses by tomorrow noon it will be difficult." I started feeling dizzy. I sat down on the sofa and started crying. Anisha sat next to me and rolled her arm around my shoulder. She tried comforting me. "She is going to be ok Satyam. We can only pray." It was becoming impossible to stop my tears. I started crying profusely. It was me who was responsible for all this mess but I could not tell this to anyone. "Have you eaten anything?" she asked. I waved my head. "Come let us go to the canteen," she suggested. "No, I don't feel like eating," I told her. "Come yaar, there is nothing we can do right now. You need to conserve your energy if you want to be by her side when she wakes up tomorrow. Come have a coffee and some light snacks," she pulled my arm without even waiting for me to reply. I did not say anything and started following her.

It was almost after two years that we were meeting face to face. Who would have thought that our first meeting after such a long gap would be like this. We sat at the coffee table facing each other. She had not changed a bit. She was the same old Anisha of college days. "Why did she take such an extreme step?" she asked. I did not know what to tell her. I could not lie to her and I could not even tell the whole truth. "She got dumped," I told her. "But such an extreme step? The guy must have used her badly." I did not reply. "Someone from her family should be here. Do you have any contact numbers? We should call her family members," she suggested. "She does not have any family. Only friends," I replied. "Oh, that is why she is emotionally so weak. Her boy friend knows she did this?" "Yes, he does," I replied. "Still he is not here. What type of person he would be?" she commented. I kept quiet. There was nothing I could say.

Her phone rang. I did not know who was on the other end but I could make out that whoever it was, that person wanted her to go back to home and she was telling that person that she could not leave me alone. The interaction lasted for some five minutes and in the end she abruptly kept the phone down. "Who was it?" I asked. "Martin," she replied. I had already guessed it would be him and though I know what transacted over the phone still I asked, "What was he saying? Is there any problem?" "No, nothing at all," she replied. She did not want to discuss that. "If you want to leave, you can go. I will be fine," I told her. "Don't be stupid. How can I leave you in such a situation?" she argued. "But Martin wants you back home. And anyway it is too late in the night," I told her. "To hell with whatever he wants, I am not going anywhere. I can take care of myself and anyway you are here so I don't need to worry about anything," she still did not understand why Martin wanted her to come back. "I am here, that is why Martin wants you to go back," I added some fuel to fire. "What do you mean?" she asked. The moment she was finished her phone rang. "Talk to him, it is Martin," I told her without looking at the phone. It was Martin and this time they had a hot altercation. "I don't know what has happened to him. He was never so bossy before. I do not know why he is behaving like this today," she commented once she hung up the phone. I did not reply to her. I just smiled. "What do you mean?" she asked. She knew what I meant so I did not reply. She also kept quiet for some time and then she asked, "Do you think Martin has problem with us?" "Well... with time you will know yourself," I replied. "No, I don't want to know myself. I want you to tell me," she argued. "There is nothing I can tell you. Only time can tell what is right and what is wrong." She was not satisfied with my answer and again asked, "Satyam, tell me one thing. Am I doing any mistake in marrying him? Tell me frankly whatever you feel. You know me and you are the only person who can tell me this. I am still not convinced about marrying him. Tell me, am I committing a mistake?" This was my golden moment. This was the time I could have told her that what all she felt was wrong. She would never get that much freedom with

Martin. She would have to make compromises at every step. She would not be able to live the life the way she wanted to. I was amazed why she could not see all that herself. It was so clear to me. Before I could speak a ward boy came to us. He talked to Anisha, "Ma'am, your patient is getting back to senses." We ran towards the ICU. The doctor told us that Zora was out of danger. He did not allow us to go inside and meet her. We will have to wait for that till tomorrow. It was a big relief. We stood at the ICU gate and I could see her. Her eyes were open. She was looking at me and she was smiling. I could not match her gaze and lowered my head.

We again went to the coffee house. I was much relieved now. She was out of danger. I could not forget her look. I was responsible for all her troubles. Anisha asked me again, "You have not answered me. Tell me, am I doing any mistake in marrying him?" "No, you are not. He is the perfect match for you," I replied. She did not accept my answer, "how can you say that? Even now when we are not married he has problems with me meeting with you. I don't know how he will behave after we are married." "It is ok for him to feel jealous yaar. After all he is going to be your husband. He would definitely not like you to be with a stranger at 3 A.M. in the night," I told her. "But you are not a stranger. You are my best friend and he knows that," she argued. "But I am your best friend, not his. To him I am a stranger," I wanted her to realize what was true. "But then I have my own life," she was her old self, still believing that everything will work the way she wants it to work. "Once you get married you will not have your own life. You will have shared life." "I don't want to get married in that case," she told firmly. "Don't be stupid, you people are already engaged and your marriage date is also fixed. Don't talk stupid things," I told her. "I am not talking stupid things Satyam. I am still not convinced if I am making the right choice in marrying him," she looked down as she said that. "But why are you having doubts now? It is already too late to have any doubts," I asked her. She did not reply. She kept looking down. Tears trickled down from her eyes as she said, "Satyam, I think I love you."

For the last three years I had been waiting to hear that one line from her mouth and when she said it I was in such a situation that I could not do anything. Zora was on her death bed because of me. It was my responsibility to take care of her now. I could not react, I could not speak anything. This was the most desperate situation that I could ever be in Anisha was sitting in front of me, telling me that she loved me and I could not accept that, I could not tell her how much I had waited to hear that one line, how much I loved her, how I would be willing to give my life just to be with her. But now it was not the question of my life alone, it was the question of Zora's life as well. I had no right over that and I could not sacrifice her life just to be with my love.

"Are you nuts? You are going to get married in two weeks and you are telling me you love me?" "Yes, I do. I know it now. I want to marry you, not him. Will you marry me?" she asked. She had spoken so much in those five seconds for which I would have happily waited for centuries. How I wished that she would have realized that earlier. "What are you saying stupid? We are friends, not lovers. And just because Martin wants you home does not mean that you should not marry him. Had I been in his place I would have done the same," I know I was lying to her but that was the best thing I could do at that moment. She took my hand in her hands and asked me, "tell me you don't love me," she was crying. "No, I don't love you," I told her. She kept looking at my face. She was still holding my hand, crying. "Anisha, I agree we do flirt at times, but that is just healthy flirting. I do not love you yaar, I just flirt with you. Come on now. Be a game yaar. Isn't flirting fun?" It was indeed difficult but it was for everyone's good. Many a times I had lied before, this time as well I was perfect. She threw back my hand, "you should not have played with my heart," she said and then she ran away.

45

Zora was out of danger now. She had been shifted from ICU to the normal ward. I was allowed to meet her now. She was semi-conscious, still under the effect of barbiturates. I sat next to her pillow and slowly caressed her forehead with my hand. She opened up her eyes. She looked at me and smiled, "I knew you would come." "Of course stupid, why would not I come? And how could you even think of taking such a step dear. You are totally mad,' I told her. She did not speak any thing. She just smiled back at me. "I love you," she said. "I know that dear," I told her. She closed her eyes and again went to sleep.

    She kept moving in and out of consciousness for another day. By the end of second day, she was completely out of danger. Anisha had not come back even once after I told her that I did not love her. That was good for all of us. Meeting her would not be good for Zora and I was not in a condition to leave Zora alone.

"I am sorry." This was the first time in three days when Zora was speaking in full consciousness. "Sorry for what?" I asked her. "You know for what, I have given you a lot of pain. I should know how to live with failures. I can not just have my way always," she spoke as tears rolled down her cheeks. "Shut up stupid, you just get healthy and don't bother about anything else. We will bother about other things later," I told her. "Don't worry Satyam. I know you do not love me. Don't bother about me. I will not attempt my life again. I will live without you. Trust me I can do that," she spoke. "How are you feeling now?" I tried to change the topic. "A lot better, who brought me here?" she asked. "Anisha," I replied. She did not look at me and she did not reply. She closed her eyes.

Zora was discharged on the next day. I took her to her home and made her settle down there. My mid term exams were going to start in two days. I had to go back but I was worried lest she might attempt her life again. I decided to talk to her clearly about this, "Zora promise me you will never do this stupidity again. I will do whatever makes you happy." "It is not a question of my happiness alone Satyam, your happiness is also interlinked," she argued. "And you think I would have lived happily if something would have happened to you? If this is what you are going to do then let us get married." If that was the only thing that would give her a reason to live then I was ready to give it a chance. "No Satyam, I do not want you to make any sacrifice for me. I do not want you to marry me out of mercy. If ever we get married

I want that to happen because both of us want to do that, not because I forced you to," she continued, "I know what you must be thinking. You must be thinking that if I actually think so then why I attempted suicide. No Satyam, I swear on Allah, I did not do that to pressurize you into marrying me or to make you feel guilty. I did this because I was weak, because it came as a shock to me, because I did not know how I will be able to live without you. I am sorry for that." She rested her head in my lap. She was crying silently. I started caressing her head. After a while she spoke again, "Satyam, I promise you I will not attempt my life again and I promise that I will never force you to marry me again. In case you ever feel like marrying me, promise me that you will tell me. I will wait for you my whole life." I did not trust a single word of what she was saying. She was telling that because she was emotionally disturbed then. Once I get married to someone else she would definitely move on. As far as the question of committing suicide was concerned, if she had tried that once she could attempt that again and the biggest priority I had was to ensure that she does not do that again. "Let us talk about something else for the time being. Let us give each other some time but promise me that you will never attempt your life again. Promise me that even if such a thought comes in your mind ever you will just let me know and not do anything stupid," I held her hand and asked her to commit me. She promised.

I stayed with her till evening. We discussed many things but not our relationship. In the evening I left for Calcutta. There was a lot of preparation to be done for mid-terms and very little time.

THE END OF THE BEGINNING

46

I was in two minds, whether to call Anisha and tell her the truth or not. I could not figure out the right path for myself so I decided to discuss with Rick. I shared everything with him, from beginning till end. How it started, how I had met Zora, the dynamics between Avash - Anisha, Anisha - me, me - Avash, Zora - me and what had happened in the last week. By the end of recounting all this I was even more confused than I was before. Rick heard everything. We discussed over & over again coming back to the same point. We had an exam to write the next day. Though I had already given up on it, I was wasting Rick's time too. Rick suggested that I give myself some time till the exams were over and probably I would get some clarity by then. But I did not have much time. If I waited for long Anisha would be gone forever, if I did not Zora might attempt her life and I would live a life full of guilt. 'Sometimes the best you can do is to do nothing. Let God take care of things from here on,' this was the last suggestion that came from Rick before he left for his room to study. This was not something I wanted to do. I did not believe that God would have enough time to bother about me but there was nothing much that I could do than resign myself to fate. Believers say that God always has a plan, whatever happens is for good of all. For once I decided to believe in it.

I did not get any chance to prepare for the exams. As such, I had lost all interest in that mad race for grades and jobs. There were bigger things in life than these, things where I had already gained some and lost much. I just wanted to scrape through the exams but with the efforts I had put in even that seemed difficult. Exams were over and results were declared. I did not even bother to check my marks. Every day I would wait for my cell phone to ring, every time it rang I would take the call anticipating I would get to hear from Anisha, each time I would be disappointed. Then one fine day, she called but it was a bit too late. It was the day she was getting married. "You have left me alone on this day and you did not even care to give me a call today?" she complained. I could not utter a word. I always knew she would not marry without talking to me. I wanted her to talk. I wanted to hear her voice. I wanted to know that she was happy but she was not. I could make that out from her voice. She did not speak a word after that. Neither did I. But we were communicating; we knew what was going on inside us. That was the most beautiful and most perfect conversation one could have had but then sometimes silence is not sufficient, sometimes you want to hear it out even if you know it is true. "One last time please," she requested. I could not turn her down. "I love you," I replied. We both were crying now. After a while she asked, "Then why…" I had asked that question to myself many a times but I had not been able to find any answer. What answer could I offer her? "Zora," I replied. We did not talk after that. In that one moment I lost my best friend and the love of my life but there was nothing I could do. I do not know why things turned out the way they did. Things could have happened differently. All of us would have been much happier but now all of us were leading half lives. We all were incomplete. Was this best for all? No one will ever know.

Meanwhile my relationship with Zora had become more of a formality. Every other day she would give me a call and tell about what all was happening in her life. I would just reply in yes, no and ok. She had stopped complaining now. Either she had accepted the way things were or she still believed that once Anisha would get married I would start feeling for her. Whatever it may be, it had more or less become a routine activity. Neither did she stop calling me nor I would ever upset her by not taking her calls. One thing was sure that she still loved me a lot.

I wrote my end term exams and again flunked in Statistics – II. This was not a surprise at all. I knew it would happen. What was actually a surprise was the fact that I had cleared all other courses. The way I had fared in the exams I was expecting my days in the institute to be over.

47

The best thing about failing in a relationship is that you get a lot of sympathy from your friends. This lets people come closer and builds a lasting bond. Something similar was happening between Rick and me. During my tough time he supported me. I had started spending more and more time with him and the more I did that the more praises I had for his outlook towards life. He was not dependent on anyone for his emotional needs. I had asked him once what his secret was. 'Diversify your portfolio *baccha*. You talk to only one girl that is why you get dependent on her. I talk to so many of them that there is no way one of them becomes too important for my emotional needs. Love is nothing but a glorified term for emotional needs. No law says you have to share all your emotions with only one person. Never let anyone become so important in your life that your happiness or sorrow is determined by that person.' I feel he was right. Even if he was wrong he was happy. It was worth taking a chance.

I called up Jhilmil but could not get through. Probably her number had changed. I left her a one line mail asking if she wanted to talk. In the evening she pinged me.
What is it?
I am missing you.
Don't lie please.
No, really I am missing you. I think you are cute.
Liar ☺
Trust me dear. I was busy with my exams so could not contact for long. And anyway you are single now. Right?
Yes right. So?
So, do you think we should meet?
What if I say no?
I will keep on asking until you say yes.
But why?
Because you are so cute.
You are a perfect flirt
Only when I am chatting with you sweetheart
Ok ☺
So when and where?
 Sunday, at 11, my home.
This time your bf won't come?
No. This time am all yours
And so it was all set. I was on my way to recovery.

48

After her marriage I had thought that I will lose touch with Anisha. Indeed she did not call me for a month. But I was wrong. She did contact me. She had mailed me her marriage and honeymoon pictures. She was looking beautiful in those pictures. It was a cute couple. They did look happy together. I guess I was wrong or might be it was just the honeymoon period. I wrote a reply to her mail offering my wishes. She did not want to break the link and neither did I. I did not know how we would react if we would meet face to face again but as long as the communication was restricted to mails and chats I did not foresee many problems between us.

Irrespective of whatever the future held for us I had my own plans. I wanted to become the master of my emotions again and had already taken the first step towards it. This

Sunday I was ready to take the giant step. I woke up at six, took out my jogging shoes and stepped out. I jogged for around half an hour and then went to the jetty. I stood there for some time watching the fish under the water. When it started getting hot I moved towards my hostel room. I was all set to be a changed man. I took a warm shower and groomed myself for the encounter. What was in store today meant much more than just a casual encounter. Though we had tried meeting earlier as well but that was different. Then, it was the excitement, the adrenaline rush, the thrill of doing something that was not generally accepted. This time it was more about proving a point; to no one else but to me. It would be symbolic of my victory over the past; it would provide me the much needed detachment from my emotions.

I gave Jhilmil a final call to confirm the appointment before leaving from the hostel. It was all set as per the plan. I reached her place in time and rang her door bell. Instead of opening the door she gave me a call. She told me that the door was unlatched and I should come inside. 'Was she again getting ready for the shower?' I started wondering. As the moment was coming near I could feel a little excitement building inside me. I stepped inside and latched the door behind me. I headed straight towards her room. She was lying on the bed draped with a silky white sheet. She gave me a beautiful smile. I went to her bed and without asking for permission sat by her side. We both knew why we were there and so no permission was required. "How are you doing?" I asked her more out of formality then concern but it should have been the other way out. "Not well. I have been suffering from viral fever since last two days. I am feeling extremely tired," she told me.

This was something I had not expected this time. I did not know what to do. Whether to make the first move or not? I decided to wait for her to make the first move. Moreover I wanted to be sure that she was ready for it. We started talking and continued to talk. Hours kept passing by and talking was all we did. I did not want to appear desperate and so I continued entertaining her boring talks. By the end of two hours I was sure that nothing would come out of it. There was no point in just sitting there and wasting my time. I decided to take her leave. She came till the gate to see me off. She opened the door to let me move out. The moment I stepped out of the door I found a guy standing there. Instead of closing the door behind me Jhilmil stepped out and started talking to the guy, "What are you doing at my gate? You are still spying on me? I have already told you that I am going around with Satyam. Leave me alone now." The guy looked at me and then looked at her, "You should not have done this." He was almost in tears as he spoke, "Satyam will never love you. He is just using you. You will know it when it will be too late." He told that and he left.

All this happened so fast that I was taken aback. I did not have any chance to speak or express anything. After he left I turned back to Jhilmil and told her to move inside. She refused. She did not appear sick at all. I was confused at her behaviour. "Will you please tell me what is going on?" I asked her, "And will you please let me step in so that we can sit and talk?" "What is there to talk about?" she smiled. "You had told me that you people had broken off." I looked at her for an answer. "Indeed we have broken up, did not you see that," she started laughing now. I understood what was going on. She was not at all sick. She was not dumb at all as I had thought. Rather she was way too smart for me. She had intentionally left her passwords with her boy friend so that he knows when I am with her. I was just being used by her to get rid of that guy. "How could you do that Jhilmil? You have used me," I expressed my anguish. "Yes, you can very easily dream of sleeping with me when you don't even know me. You think I am too dumb, you would very easily use me and I would not even realize that. There was nothing wrong in that. Now when it is not you but me who turns out to be the smart one you are asking me how can I do that? Ask this question to yourself Mr. Satyam and don't try to contact me again ever," she said that and then she banged the door on my face.

Things did not turn out the way I had planned. I quietly came back to my hostel. Someone had said it right. 'There are no free lunches.' Not only lunches. There are no free dinners or breakfast or even snacks for that matter. With Jhilmil I was hoping to get free dinner however I ended up washing the dishes. Her boy friend will always think that it was me who was responsible for their break-off. I would live under constant worry of expecting retaliation while she would go on flirting with new persons at will. She was a genius indeed. If I would have been only half as smart as she was, Anisha would have been with me by now.

49

Third term was much more difficult as compared to the previous terms. Though during the second term I had lost all hope of completing the course but when I managed to pass the exams with just one failure I realized that I still had a chance. If I could somehow manage to pass all the exams in third term I could easily survive in the college. Fourth term onwards we get to choose the subjects by our own choice so there was no question of choosing any math based subject again and putting my future in peril. It was just the third term that I had to manage somehow.

After the learning Jhilmil gave me I did not try such encounters again. Meanwhile Zora had also found her peace with life. She no longer used to call me on alternate days. The frequency had now reduced to once a week however the content of the conversation still did not change. She will talk about her life and I will keep on listening till she felt bored of speaking. We never fought again. It was a peaceful relationship which she kept on dragging because she was still in love. It was not that I was happy for her. I was not happy at the pain she was undergoing and the way our relationship was shaping up. I was losing a friend and the same was true for her. I did talk to her about this a couple of times but she always silenced me by asking if I can have one sided love for Anisha and still be friends with her why can not the same happen between us. She did not realize that the same was happening between us until she took that dire step and I could not allow the same to happen again for I can not take any chances on her life. I sincerely wished that she would find someone someday who would love her as much as she would love him but whenever I told her this she would say that before she would ever love anyone else she will have to stop loving me which could never happen. The same was true for me. I felt that I would never fall out of love with Anisha and so there never would be a question of loving someone else. Even though she had been married for months now but I was still in love with her.

It was a few weeks before my final exams when Anisha pinged me on chat. Though we had been communicating on mails till now but they were more or less formal in nature. Many a times I saw her online but I never initiated the conversation. How could I start? She still meant the world to me however I did not know how she felt about me. She was leading a normal life and she did seem happy, as such it would not be right if I burden her with my troubles. This time she had pinged to share her troubles. We exchanged greetings. Initially she was not opening up but when I prodded further she could not contain herself anymore.

He does not understand me at all. You were right, I was mistaken.

Have you talked to him in detail?

Yes, I have. But he does not want me to go. If I say no to my company this time they might not give me any further chance.

Anisha's company was sending her to London for three months to work on the client site but Martin had problems with that. He was not giving her any reasons as to why he did not want her to go. He had just told her that she should not go.

Why don't you reason it out with him?

Do you think I have not tried that? He is not ready to listen to anything. He expects me to be an Indian wife. He wants me to quit the job and take care of household chores.

Bull shit. Since how long has this been happening?

Ever since we got married.

Why did not you tell me earlier?

What should have I told you? I never realized your importance when you were with me. What can I say now?

Can I ask one thing?

Yes.

Do you still love me?

She did not reply to my question. Instead she changed the topic. In case she would have replied I would have taken her answer with an element of doubt but her silence confirmed me beyond doubt that she did feel for me. She was not happy with Martin. As such I did not see any reason as to why she should stay with him. That day I did not discuss anything about it further but I did push her to stick to her stand and to continue working. She promised me that she will try her best.

Same evening she had called me. She was crying. She had had a bitter fight with Martin. He had told her that under no circumstances would he allow her to continue disregarding his feelings. He wanted her to be a housewife. He had told her that there was no point in continuing her job once she becomes a mother. She was very weak and Martin was responsible for this. Why could he not understand that they were two different individuals and she had a right to make her own decisions, just like he made all of his. Somewhere I too was responsible for her condition. I could have stopped her from marrying him. She used to always consult with me. It was always in my hands but I never did that. I wanted her to make her own decision even when I knew it would be a wrong one. That day both of us kept crying on the phone. She was blaming herself for my state and I was blaming myself for the troubles that she was facing. We wanted to meet desperately but that was not possible now. We had written our destinies ourselves and now we had no escape, we had to endure that under all circumstances.

Slowly it turned into a routine affair. Anisha would call me daily and we would talk for around an hour or so. Though it was never something specific that we used to discuss but we never seemed to run out of conversations. I was again beginning to get interested in life and she too seemed happier talking to me. Martin had finally allowed her to go to London but on the pre condition that she will quit her job and take up the household chores after this assignment. She had resigned to her fate. There was a time when we used to believe that we will be the master of our own destiny but now it seemed that resigning to fate had become a habit with both of us. However we still wanted to show it as an outcome of our own choice, may be just to get some solace in the feeling that it is still us and no one else who is controlling our actions. Whatever it was, we were content in talking, sharing our sorrows and joys together. Martin did not know that we were on talking terms. We both knew that he would never understand us and would never approve of us having any contact so there was no point in sharing all this with him. If he would have understood Anisha these problems would never have materialized in the first place.

50

The end term exams were over. Results were yet to be declared but the summer internship program was about to begin. Successfully completing the first year was a compulsory requirement for taking the internship but since the results were scheduled a bit late we were temporarily allowed to begin with our internship. Rick and I travelled together to Heathrow. I would continue my journey towards Norway from there. Our flight to Heathrow was an eleven hour journey. During the journey we kept talking about different things and after some time the topic shifted to Anisha. Initially I was reluctant to talk about her but when Rick prodded me I told him everything. He was under the impression that after she got married we would have broken all contact but when he got to know the truth he was jubilant. "She still loves you *yaar*," he told me. "Tell me something I don't know," I replied. He felt surprised at my emotionless reply, "Are not you happy about it?" "No, this is even more painful. Earlier at least I could console myself by thinking that it was a one sided feeling but now I know it is not and still I can not do anything but just miss her. Though she is mine but still she is not mine. This is the worst form of pain one can get in a relationship but you would not understand," I had told him. "But who tells you to endure all this pain? When you both are in love why don't you start a new life together?" I don't know whether he had even thought for a second before he uttered those words but I had definitely not given it a thought earlier. For a moment I was taken aback but then the idea did seem worth some thought. "What are you hinting at?" I asked Rick. Rick stared at me for some time. He was trying to gauge my reaction but I did not show any expression. He understood I wanted him to talk and so he started speaking, "You are not dumb not to get it. You already know what I am hinting at. You will be in Norway for next two months and she will be coming to London next week. You will get at least eight weekends to spend with her. This much time is sufficient for you to convince her to get a divorce. You can live happily ever after." "Have you gone mad? Do you have any idea what you are talking about?" I was still not convinced if Rick had clearly thought about it or it was just a comment he had made. "Ok, leave it then if you feel so, anyway you do not have the guts to do that." Rick said that and put on his earphones. He started watching a movie. He was in no mood to talk now but he left me thinking. During the entire journey I kept thinking about what he said.

51

'A fresh start... would it be possible? Though it would not be that difficult for me but I could not say that about her with surety. She had a family now. Will she be willing to leave them all for me? At least we were talking now and we were closer than before. Was it really worth risking all that? I kept thinking on these lines for a few days, sometimes it felt like this was the right thing to do while at others it seemed like it would be a selfish decision and I should not do that. If we did choose to start a new life it would not only affect the two of us but also Anisha's family, her in-laws, Zora and Avash as well. Every time I would start thinking about it I would not be able to continue and stop midway thinking of all these issues.'

My internship had started. Anisha was supposed to come to London in a week's time. We had decided against

communicating on phone as it would be very costly for us. She had told me she will meet me online at 4 PM India time daily and she did keep her promise. We continued to chat regularly and both of us were excited about meeting in Europe. Finally one day I decided to talk to her about us and the new beginning.
What do you think we will do in London?
I don't know. And as long as I am with you I don't even care. This might be the last time we get to meet together and I would love to cherish every moment of it.
Do you really want it to be the last time we would meet?
No.
Then why don't we do something about it?
What can we do?
Don't you think we should spend our life together?
Forget it Satyam. If we could always get what we want, this world would have been a different place altogether.
It is not about the world it is about the two of us, the world can take care of itself.
What is the use of wishing something when we know it can not happen? You are making me cry Satyam.
Do you love me?
What do you mean?
Give me an answer. Do you love me?
Why are you asking this?
Do you love me?
Don't you know the answer?
I know the answer but I want to know from you. Tell me do you love me?

Yes.
Will you marry me?
What are you saying Satyam? How is it possible?
It is possible. First tell me are you ready for it?
No.
Why? Don't you trust me?
You know Satyam it is not like that. I do trust you but I am already married.
But are you happily married?
Why are you asking this?
Do you want to spend your entire life like this? Anisha don't just give up. This is all we have done throughout. This is one last time when we have got a chance, let us for once decide our own lives, for once we should write our own destiny. One last chance to ourselves...
Is it possible?
Yes, but only if we want to make it possible.
What will I have to do?
Nothing, just remember to keep all your important documents with you when you come here because you will never go back to that house again.
I am not sure if I understand that.
Both of us will be here for a couple of months. We will file for your divorce from here. Martin can not do anything until we are here. Two months will be enough to get divorce. Anyway he would not want to stay with you any longer once he will know you are with me.
But what about mom, will she approve of it?
Are you currently living with your mom?

No.
Then it should not matter and anyway she will only want to see you happy in the long run. She might get angry initially but that might not last for long.
What about Avash and Zora?
Anisha whole of our lives we have been thinking about others. Let us for once think about ourselves first. In any case you are not going to marry Avash and I am not going to marry Zora so there is no point staying away because of them.
I don't know what to say. It is happening so fast, I can not think.
You don't need to think. You just need to have faith. Do you trust me?
Yes, I do.
Then for once, let me decide for us. Please.
Ok. Tell me what should I do?
Sunday, 11 AM, meet me at Virgin's store in Oxford Street.
What will we do?
We will go to Germany from there. No one will be able to guess that we will be in Germany. We will stay there until you get divorce.
But what about my job?
You were anyway going to leave that so don't bother about it. Once we are back you can join some other firm.
And what about your internship?
You are much more important than any internship. I will give a medical and complete the internship next year. Don't worry about that.

Do you think this will work out?
Tell me, do you love me?
Yes I do.
Do you trust me?
Yes I do.
Then leave all your worries to me. Everything will work out.

That day we decided to give ourselves another chance. Though it should have happened much earlier but even if this was happening so late we were happy about it. There was no question of having any regrets. No one ever forced us to do something. Whatever decisions we had ever made; whether by our own will or by leaving it to destiny, in the end it was our own choice. No one ever forced a decision on us. Even when we had decided to do nothing it was a choice we had consciously made. There was no question of regretting the choices that turned out wrong. Also there was no point in binding ourselves to the consequences of those choices just because we had made those decisions ourselves. It is never too late to admit a mistake. No one is perfect, we certainly were not. We had made wrong choices in the past and now it was the time to rectify them. Who knows the choice we were making now would also be wrong but we would never know until that happens and in the end if we do find out that it was a wrong choice still we would be better off. We would be better off because instead of submitting to the destiny we tried, we would be better off because instead of continuing to lead the painful life we would get to spend at least a few more days of pleasure, a few more days of excitement which only we would be able to share, which would stay with us for a lifetime, we would be better off because if we do find out that it was a wrong decision we would not be afraid to risk everything once again and we would not be afraid to start a new life.

52

Next couple of days I kept busy planning for the big step. A lot of things needed to be done. Rick helped me out in locating a budget accommodation & making our travel arrangements. The plan was all set. Saturday night I would be moving to Rick's place. Sunday noon I will meet Anisha & Sunday night we will take an overnight train to Germany. I had not planned about how things will move forward once we reach Germany but I had faith that things will workout.

Saturday evening my internship supervisor called me in his office. He handed me a white envelope. It was from my university. The envelope was addressed to my supervisor. I took out the letter & started reading it. My worst fear was confirmed. This was intimation from my university to the firm that I had failed to clear the first year. I was not eligible to undertake internship. I read the letter completely, folded it back across its edges & kept it inside the envelope. I kept the envelope at supervisor's table & turned back to move out of his office. He called me back. The ordeal was not yet over. He handed me over another envelope. It contained my return tickets to India. If I was not going to do internship I had no reason to stay in Europe at company's expense. I was supposed to leave Europe within 24 hours. I was booked on a Sunday evening flight to India.

After coming back to my hotel room I tried to search for the results on university's website but in our university results were only displayed on notice board. Neither there were any results on the university portal nor any information about the result being declared. I called Vishal – the student representative for Academic Affairs. He confirmed the bad news. Thirteen students were going to repeat a year & five were asked to withdraw permanently from the program, me being one of them. I asked him how it had happened, which subject I had flunked in but he did not remember that. All he remembered was that I was one of the five who would never step into campus again.

Things were happening quite fast. There was not enough time to think let alone brood. I now had two tickets to Heathrow, one for the evening flight that I had booked & the other one for the Sunday morning flight that the company had booked. I had already packed all my stuff so I decided to stick to the original plan & left for Rick's place.

After meeting Rick I told him about the results. Even he was not aware that the results had been declared. He felt sorry for me but result was not the part that was bothering me then, it was Anisha. "Rick, Do you think what we are doing is right?" "Don't mix things Satyam. Just because your result is not good does not mean that standards get changed. This is no time to think about right or wrong when you did not think about it earlier," he told me. He did not answer my question. He did not tell me whether it was right or wrong. He just told me not to think about it. "It means you feel that it is wrong?" "No, not at all; Satyam, since when did we people start thinking about right or wrong? Who defines right or wrong and with whose consent? You are just following your heart & it is never a sin to follow your heart. Don't bother about anything now, just follow your heart." In a way he was right. What is right or wrong, only some parameters imposed by a few on many others. If some act of mine does not make me feel good does it really matter if that was the purest thing to do. "No Rick, I am not discussing the moral part of it. Try to think practically, things are different now. I am an IIM thrown out. What future do I have now? I might not be able to get even my old job back. On top of that I have taken tons of loans for this bull shit MBA. Till yesterday my future was secure. Today I don't have any future. Do you think Anisha will still go with me after knowing all this?" Rick gave me a look of disgust. "You mean Anisha is eloping with you because you had an IIM tag? If that be the case then forget her." He had misunderstood my comment. "I did not mean that yaar. I know Anisha loves me unconditionally & any tag does not matter with her but think practically I would not be able to provide financial security to her now. I know things are going to be painful & I also know that she will endure all this pain without blinking an eyelid but does she deserve all that?" I said that & started looking down. I was getting really confused. It was now when I was speaking all this that I actually realized the implications of my failure. He understood what I was going through. He spoke softly, "If you are that worried then discuss it with Anisha before taking any step. Meet her tomorrow, discuss things with her & then let her decide what she wants. Don't influence her decision in any case, just tell her the facts, tell her what you think & then let her decide for herself."

That seemed the only right thing to do at that moment. That night I could not sleep. I kept thinking about Anisha. I could not give myself a reason not to be with her & I also could not find a reason to force her into all the troubles that lay in her path with me. The more I thought the more confused I was. I kept thinking over & over but without any results.

53

In the morning I had a light breakfast. I bid goodbye to Rick & took a taxi to Oxford Street. We had discussed it over breakfast again. I would meet Anisha & tell her everything, what had happened & what hardships she might face in future. I will let her make an informed choice.

I reached Oxford Street at a quarter before eleven. We had not contacted each other after that chat. It would be difficult to locate each other in such a market place so I decided to wait outside the store. After half an hour she came. The moment I saw her I waved my hand. She smiled. I smiled back. In a moment I forgot all the tensions & confusions that were running in my mind. One look at her face & I knew we had to be together. She handed me a piece of paper. I took it & looked at her questioningly but she did not react. I started reading.

'I know when I will be in front of you I would not be able to speak anything, I would not be able to think of anything else but you & so I am writing this down.

I am the luckiest person in this world. It is difficult to find one's love in a lifetime. After I got married I thought I am one of those unlucky ones who live there lives without ever knowing what is love but it is because of you that now I know what it means to be in love. You were always there for me, even today you are ready to accept me & leave everything for my sake. You know Satyam, you are powerful & you are the source of my power too. If today I have been able to prepare myself to leave everything behind & give myself another chance it is not because of me. It is because of you, because I know no matter what happens you will always be there to take care of me. With you life always seems simple but without you it is full of complexities. I know no one else will ever be able to take care of me the way you will do but still there is something that is stopping me from taking this plunge.

For once I tried to think about what all I was leaving behind when I come with you. It was not much. A few bad memories, a few intimate relations, a few quarrels, a few blessings & other little things. I thought I would be able to leave all these behind me & will make a completely new start but there are a few things that will always remain with me & remind me of my past. I do not bother about what we are doing is right or wrong as long as it affects only me but here it will affect others too. Not the ones who are apart but the one who is my own part, who is sensing life inside me. It is not only my life I am responsible for. I want to keep my child & I don't know if I would be able to take care of it. I know you will take care of my child just like you care about me but does it really deserve to be away from its father? Does Martin deserve never to take his child in his own arms, never to hear its voice?

I thought over & over but I have no answers to these questions. I am not strong at all. I can not decide for myself. I know whatever you decide will be for good of both of us. I want you to decide for both of us.

If you love me & are willing to accept my child then tear this letter apart & take me with you. I will always be with you in your thick & thin.

If you feel what we are doing is not right then please turn back & leave. Don't speak a single word. Don't look at me or I would not be able to stop you from going.

Thanks for being a part of my life. I love you. I will always do.'

I looked up at her face. We did not exchange a single word. She had tears trickling down her cheeks. I kept looking at her for a while. She lowered her head & started crying. She did not deserve those tears. I wiped her tears with my hand. She looked up, her face emotionless. I moved closer to her & kissed her. She stood quietly looking into my eyes. I tore the letter to pieces, and then I moved back, picked up my luggage, turned around & stopped a taxi. "Airport Please."